The Village Narcissist

Glenis Kellet

"The Village Narcissist, will hold you in its grip until the very end of the book, and you'll be wanting more as it finally comes to its conclusion!"

– Maurean Hoyle

First published in Great Britain as a softback original in 2020

Typeset in Adobe Garamond Pro

Editing, design, typesetting and publishing by UK Book Publishing

www.ukbookpublishing.com

ISBN: 978-1-913179-60-1

THE
VILLAGE
NARCISSIST

I dedicate this book to all who have been affected by the COVID-19 global pandemic and particularly to those who have sadly died prematurely from this terrible virus.

THE DISCOVERY

A shrill piercing scream vibrated through the still, silent air. A plump middle-aged woman ran down the wooden steps from the bell tower – breathless and terrified at what she had just witnessed. She ran into the nave of the old church, running towards the voices and hurried steps she had heard coming from the vestry.

"There's a woman hanging from a bell rope," she screamed, pointing back to the way she had come. Her face was ashen in colour due to her terrible shock; she visibly shook from the sight of the horrific scene.

The four men looked at each other in total surprise!

"Ring the police!" she frantically cried. She was stunned at their behaviour – why were they just stood there doing nothing? She thought to herself.

The Vicar tried to calm her. "Come with me, I'll make you a strong cup of tea, let these men see to her and ring the police, you must have had a nasty shock!"

She heard the three men run up the wooden steps as she and the kind young vicar walked out of the church.

"Shouldn't I stay for the police, they'll want to interview me?" the frightened woman asked.

"Don't worry, the men will tell them where we are," he gently reassured her.

They walked towards a house nearby; the sign on the tall, wrought iron gate had the words 'THE NEW VICARAGE' written in bold black letters on it. There was a lovely old rambling building at the back of the house.

"Was that other house, the original vicarage?" she asked, trying to take her troubled mind off the body hanging from the bell rope.

"Yes, it was, but this house is more manageable. Come in and sit yourself down, I'll pop the kettle on." He left to go to the kitchen and she sat in a comfortable armchair, still trembling from her ordeal. The room was full of tall, old fashioned bookcases crammed with books on theology. A long-carved table stood in the middle of the room with 10 chairs placed around it – possibly where the parishioners conducted their parochial business, she thought.

"Here we are, this will help calm your nerves, what a dreadful shock you've had. We don't generally have visitors coming to our village as it's so very remote. I hope it hasn't put you off coming again!" the cheerful vicar told her.

"No, I'll come again, I didn't take the photos I wanted."

The vicar offered her a biscuit covered in a white powder, probably icing sugar, most unusual she thought.

Her hands were still trembling as she raised her cup to her lips, she definitely didn't like his choice in the brand of tea, it tasted awful and it was full of sugar. She politely drank it anyway and ate the strange biscuit.

"I came to photograph the tower; I'm very interested in bell towers. When I came to stay with my sister this morning, it was the first thing I wanted to do."

"Yes, it's a very beautiful old church, the square bell tower was added on later, I believe." They chatted some more about the old church.

She began to feel lightheaded, perhaps it's the shock, she pondered or was she suffering from a virus? She was beginning to become confused.

"I'll take you back to your car," the vicar told her, unaware of her condition. He helped her out of her seat.

"But…the…pol-police…wi-will…be…here… soon." She was feeling very strange and her words were beginning to slur.

The vicar saw her to her car parked on the grass verge; she didn't feel well at all and in a very confused state. She turned the car around and drove off down the 10-mile single tarmac road and turned onto the main road, to head back into the town. She was experiencing anxiety and began to hallucinate. The trees were walking into the road! They were like people; their roots had become legs and feet! She was horrified at the frightening spectacle evolving before her. She swerved wildly, to avoid hitting them!

****

The telephone rang loudly at the police station in the nearby town.

"Hello, I'm really worried about my sister, Christine Holmes," a woman began to explain. "She went to Deadend village this afternoon, she is very interested in bell towers and was going to go and take some photographs there. She hasn't returned! I've tried to ring her mobile phone but she must have forgotten it as it rang here!"

"Don't worry, she's probably been delayed by something or was chatting," the police officer tried to reassure her.

"We had arranged to go out to celebrate her birthday but that was four hours ago!" she exclaimed.

"I suggest you ring the vicar and see if he knows anything. They have probably been talking about the old church and forgotten the time."

She frantically rang the vicar's number several times but there was no reply. She was extremely worried for her sister's safety as the light had faded. She couldn't drive out there herself, to look for Christine, as her own car was in the garage for repairs. She decided to ring the police again.

"Hello, my sister, Christine Holmes, has still not returned home."

"I'll send someone out to take some details from you, perhaps tomorrow if someone is available. If she does return home in the meantime please let us know," came the reply.

She was dismayed at their lack of concern; she had a restless night worrying about the whereabouts of her sister.

****

"What is your sister's name and address?" the pretty young police officer asked the following day.

Details were given from the anxious sibling. She continued: "She has greying dark brown hair. She wears glasses, they have a gold coloured frame… She was wearing a dark blue anorak, red jumper, black trousers and black ankle boots."

"What kind of car was she driving and the registration number?"

"A Vauxhall Corsa, SG62… err…something, I can't remember all the registration number."

"What colour is it?"

"White, it has a dent in the car's front bumper."

"What time did she leave here? Did she appear her usual self, not depressed or anything like that?"

"No, she was a happy kind of person; she left after lunch about 1.40 pm."

"I'm sure there is a reasonable explanation, so don't worry. A police officer will go to the village and make some inquiries."

****

A policeman drove up the lonely 10-mile country road. He noticed it was the first road he had ever driven on and not met another vehicle, not even a tractor! The little old church was the first building he saw; a few hundred feet away beyond the graveyard was The New Vicarage. There were fields on the opposite side of the road.

"Knock, knock."

The young vicar opened the door.

"Hello, I'm making some inquiries about a middle-aged woman who I believe came to photograph the bell tower two days ago. Did you see her at all?"

"No, I'm sorry I didn't, I was working around the church all day; if she was there, I would have seen her, I'm sure of that. Is she missing?"

The policeman replied, "Yes, her sister reported her missing."

The policeman wondered if Christine Holmes had decided to start a new life somewhere, which wasn't breaking any laws; or perhaps her sister had something to do with her disappearance. Until more details could be obtained, the case wasn't going anywhere.

Christine's sister was beside herself with worry. It was definitely not like her sister to disappear like that without telling her what was going on.

A few days later an angler was walking along the banks of a lake near to the main road. He thought he could make out the top of a white car just below the surface of the murky water. He saw there were tyre marks in the steep embankment from the road as if the car had careered off the road and travelled down into the lake below. He rang the police on his mobile phone.

It was a day's job lifting the car out of its watery grave – using a large crane brought in from elsewhere. A female body was found inside; she was still strapped into her seat belt. She was wearing a dark blue anorak, red jumper, black trousers and black ankle boots; all dripping wet. The clothed body was removed from the car and placed in a black body bag and taken away to the hospital mortuary, to be examined by the pathologist. The car was identified as Christine Holmes' car; it was a white Vauxhall Corsa, with the part registration her sister had remembered. Christine's camera was found in the foot well on the passenger side;

her gold-coloured rimmed glasses were found smashed on the pedals by her feet. Her sister was told the dreadful news – she was half expecting that something like that had happened but was still very traumatized.

The police surveyed the scene from the road. It was obvious that Christine was travelling away from Deadend village back to the town when she veered off the road. There were tyre marks suggesting she was swerving erratically. Measurements were taken and calculations made to suggest she was only travelling at about 49 miles per hour. There were now more questions than answers. Had she been to the village and no one saw her? Or did she turn around to go home as she wasn't feeling very well perhaps? Why did she veer off the road? Perhaps sheep in the road she was trying to avoid, was probably the answer.

The post-mortem revealed that Christine Holmes had drowned, her lungs were filled with muddy water. She had no alcohol in her blood or in her urine samples taken from her body, so it was determined it was an accidental death. Her sister arranged the funeral and Christine's burial took place in the town's cemetery. Her sister could only assume Christine had swerved for a rabbit or a deer and lost control of her car and it had careered down the embankment into the lake.

****

About six months later, the phone rang at the police station.

"I'm very worried about my cousin, she lives at Deadend village, I haven't heard from her in months.

She doesn't reply to phone calls, emails or letters; I live in Canada."

"Perhaps she is on a long holiday," the surly policewoman replied.

"She would have told me if she was going away on holiday, besides she didn't even send me a Christmas card and she always does!"

"If you would like to give me her name and address, we will see what we can do."

"Mrs Hilda Redford-Hamilton, she lives in The Old Vicarage."

****

The following day, a police officer entered the sleepy village. There were snowdrops in clumps dotted around the grass verges. He drove up to the old rambling house. It was a magnificent limestone building with tall chimneys on a slate roof and had steeply pitching gables; it was three storeys high. The policeman walked up to the arched doorway; he was feeling the chill in the February air. He passed a Range Rover that looked very dusty. He knocked on the oak front door. There was no reply. He walked around the old stone building, and a black cat scampered after him. It was meowing softly, its tail held high. He peered in through the windows but couldn't see Mrs Hilda Redford-Hamilton. He noticed a window at the back had been replaced – the putty around the window looked new compared to the other windows.

He drove down to the new vicarage but there was no one there, so he drove further on to a row of cottages and knocked on a brightly painted red door. A spritely lady in her eighties answered.

"Hello, I'm looking for Mrs Hilda Redford-Hamilton, I've been to her house at The Old Vicarage, but she isn't in. Do you know where I can find her?"

"Folks say she's away on a long holiday somewhere. She kept herself to herself so we don't know much about her. She moved in a few years ago, very wealthy I believe – well she must be to be able to buy a big old house like that. The upkeep must be tremendous."

"Does she own a black cat?" asked the policeman."

"Yes, come to think about it, I believe she does. She calls it Winston."

"Has she had a break-in recently? Or perhaps had a window accidently broken?"

"Not that I know of," the smart white-haired woman replied.

"Who would you go to around here to have a window replaced?"

"Alan Grey is our glazier in the village, he lives at 3, Fell View Cottages, down the road."

"Well, thank you for your time," the police officer replied.

He spoke to Alan who was eating his tea in his small kitchen – the police officer was invited in for a mug of tea. The wood burning stove's warmth was welcoming as he came in from the bitter cold wind.

"Aye, I did put the glass in window for Mrs H.R.H. – that's the nickname we give her, it's the initials of her name, it's just easier to say than her long winded posh name, Mrs Hilda Redford-Hamilton."

"Did she have a break-in?" asked the policeman.

"No, the window was cracked, probably from the frost of the winter before; it was very old glass."

"Did she employ a gardener and a cleaner?" queried the policeman.

"Aye, Fred Smith at the small cottage next door to the village hall and Lotty Sanders, the cleaner at 2, Fell Road Cottages."

He next spoke to Lotty, a tall slim woman in her 40s. She was quiet and hadn't a lot to say for herself.

"No, I've not worked for her for about six months. Not since she went on holiday."

"Where did she go on holiday and when will she return?" asked the policeman.

The woman looked away and lowered her eyes. "I don't know, she didn't tell me."

"Do you have a key to her house?"

"No," she replied. "She's always there when I go to clean, she supervises me in everything I do."

"Is that her black cat wandering about at the house, Winston is it called?"

"I think so."

"Does she normally take it to a cattery when she goes away?"

"I don't know, perhaps someone is looking after it for her."

He was suspicious, he knew she wasn't telling him all she knew.

The policeman drove up the village; he could see snow still on the fell tops. He saw the dead end in the road where the fell rose steeply almost a sheer drop from the top. It

10

was a quiet, pretty little village nestling in the foot of the fells, with about 50 houses; he knew there was zero crime rate here. It was very clean and tidy; all the gardens were immaculate apart from The Old Vicarage. There was a small fire station run by volunteers. He knew it was a well-run village and more or less self-sufficient.

There was a small school, with an old-fashioned school bell in an archway above the roof. On the opposite side of the road was a village hall which served as a pub and a post office. The school bus used the village hall car park to pick up the older children and turn around for the journey back into the town.

He drove up to the small white cottage next to the village hall. Fred was attending to his garden at the front of his cottage.

"Hello, I believe you are Fred Smith, Mrs Hilda Redford-Hamilton's gardener?" he asked.

"I am," Fred replied, getting up from a kneeling position.

"When will Mrs Redford-Hamilton return from her holiday?"

"I've no idea, she never told me she was going on holiday – that's a rumour going around the village, I think. If she's on holiday then she left me with no instructions with what to do with her garden and hasn't even paid me for work done."

"When did she leave?"

"It must have been about six months ago now, how time flies." He took off his flat cap and brushed his grey hair back with his hand and slid his cap back on.

"What kind of woman is she?"

"She's a widow – very wealthy an' aloof, not like us round 'ere."

"Does she keep herself to herself?" the policeman asked.

"Aye, mostly, she never goes to our pub nights in the village hall next door."

****

When Hilda Redford-Hamilton's cousin rang the police station from Canada, to enquire if Hilda had been found, she was dismayed at what she was told.

"She would never leave poor Winston wandering about, fending for himself while she went away on a long winter's holiday! She would have taken him to the best cattery in the area! She adored her cat."

The policeman was shocked.

"And as for – 'she kept herself to herself' – that's not my cousin at all! After two years there, she will have taken control of everything and everybody. She will have – 'shot down anyone in flames' with her curt tongue, whoever dared to resist!"

The policeman was astounded.

"I urge you to check her house, she could have had an accident or died from natural causes or something," the distraught cousin declared.

The same police officer arranged to return with a younger fellow officer, with a court order and a locksmith to access the house. They needed to investigate if she had perhaps died there. They went around the back of the large house and entered through the back door with the assistance from the locksmith. The door creaked and groaned on its rusty hinges. The black cat suddenly darted into the house, startling them.

The police officers found themselves in a whitewashed room with thick stone slabs supported on stone walls. The shutters on the small window were closed and light streamed through the cracks. Hilda's flowery patterned wellington boots were tucked underneath a stone slab with a white rattan wicker storage basket stood next to them. Hung from the hooks on the low ceiling were bunches of dried herbs and flowers. Her green gardening coat was hung on the wall hook with her white woolly hat. The floor was paved with grey stone slabs.

They went through a latched wooden door into a utility area. A row of white appliances including a large wardrobe freezer stood on the stone slabs.

"If you went away for months at a time wouldn't you empty your freezer and save electricity?" one of them asked, hearing the hum from the freezer.

"I hope she's not inside," the younger one replied looking apprehensive.

"You're joking!"

"Have a look and see." He gingerly opened the door of the freezer; it was full of frozen food and badly in need of defrosting. They both sighed with relief.

"There's washing still in the washing machine, look!"

"She's not away on holiday, that's for sure."

They entered a very large modern kitchen with a central island incorporating a breakfast bar and a fridge.

"Hilda certainly has money from somewhere to buy a place like this and keep it running." There was an unpleasant smell as they walked further into the kitchen.

They checked the fridge; the chiller had obviously iced up so much, it had forced the door ajar, the electric motor had probably burnt out as it was no longer working. Mice had got in the defrosted fridge and had made a foul smelling mess of the food inside; there was mould everywhere. They noticed there were still plates and cutlery in the washing up bowl, in the sink – showing mould growth.

"She would have emptied and washed the fridge and wouldn't have left those there, if she was going on a long holiday, surely!"

They entered an inner hallway and opened a door.

"It looks like a walk-in cupboard." It was fitted on each wall with wooden shelves from top to bottom.

"Probably an old linen cupboard – the house was used as an orphanage a long time ago." It had several artificial Christmas trees stacked up in the far corner and boxes of Christmas decorations laid on the shelves. They opened another door into a toilet area.

Another door opened into a huge walk-in pantry – what could have been pies, cakes and bread had been eaten by mice. The remains were covered in green and blue moulds. A pan of something, probably a stew, was on the side; all that was left inside the pan were mould growths. Mice had nibbled holes in the plastic containers stood in a row on the unit top. Some of the contents had spilled out – flour, pasta, rice, sugar and lentils were everywhere. Mice droppings and dead flies were littering the shelves, unit tops and the floor. A kitchen roll had been shredded by the mice to make a nest. Even the cork tops on the spherical glass jars had been eaten into and raided, dead mice still trapped inside. A plastic milk bottle had been nibbled into at the base; the milk had obviously run out onto the floor staining the flooring. There was a mouse trap with a grizzly looking dehydrated carcass of a mouse trapped by its head.

Black mould was growing on parts of the walls, ceiling and on the floor. They both put a handkerchief over their noses as the stench was overbearing. They quickly hurried out of the room. They opened a heavy door into a hallway; the house felt very cold. There was a pile of letters at the front door; one of them gathered them up and saw a few had arrived from Canada.

"These dates will perhaps tell us when she stopped reading her letters."

A smart brown coat and a cloche styled hat hung from a row of coat hooks by the door. A brown handbag stood on the ornate hall table. They examined it – her purse contained money, credit cards and her driving licence. Also, in her bag was her red spectacle case containing her glasses. There were her car keys and a small makeup bag but no mobile phone or house keys.

"She's definitely not gone on holiday; these would be the first things she would have taken with her."

"It's looking more like a death by natural causes, suicide or a homicide," replied the other officer.

A glass door led into a large dining room with a splendid candle-style chandelier hung from a large beautiful white ornate ceiling rose. In the middle of the room, there was a long oval table covered in a film of dust with twelve high backed chairs placed neatly around it. The red velvet curtains draped the mullion windows which overlooked the view at the front of the house.

Beyond the dining room was a drawing room, with sofas and chairs. There was a grand piano in one corner, with the piano keys visible. Large paintings hung on the walls in gold frames, a large black cobweb straddled two of the paintings. The house was becoming more and more eerie; they both shuddered.

Across the hallway was a large lounge with an impressive fireplace; the room was furnished and decorated in the Victorian style, rich in reds and gold. Beyond that a study – it was mainly decorated in shades of green. They could see immediately that the computer was missing, only the cables, keyboard and the printer remained on the walnut wooden desk.

"I wonder if that was why the window was broken – to steal the computer – and the glazier was lying about it?"

"Hey look here, these box files numbered one to ten – the seventh one is missing!"

"The lock on the drawer of the desk has been tampered with, someone has definitely been here and stolen things," the senior officer remarked, pulling the drawer open using his handkerchief – it was empty. "No one locks a drawer if there is nothing in it! I think forensics will have to come and see if there are any prints."

"Perhaps she caught them in the act and they killed her!" exclaimed the other.

"Hey look what I've found in this drawer, it's her passport! We can rule out that she is holidaying abroad."

The floorboards creaked, which made them feel more uneasy. Suddenly, they heard the sound of the piano playing! They looked at each other, astonished. They ran into the drawing room and looked for the mysterious piano player. There it was sat on top of the piano washing its face with its paw – it was Winston the cat!

Relieved it was nothing sinister, they went back into the hallway and climbed the sweeping wide staircase; each step groaned and creaked under their weight. They veered to the left up another five steps. They looked at each other, unnerved at what they might find. They opened the first door at the end of the gallery landing – it was an empty bedroom. The second door led into a large double bedroom, possibly Hilda's room as it was complete with furniture and summer clothes were laid carefully on the bed, with a light-coloured handbag. The chandelier crystals reflected and split the sun's rays streaming in through the window, little rainbows of light appeared on the walls around the room. A white silk dressing gown was draped over a blue and gold chaise longue. The huge double four poster bed dominated the room.

"What are you doing?" asked one of them.

"I'm looking to see if her body is under the bed, you check the wardrobe."

"Nothing here."

They both were alarmed to hear a scratching sound on the landing, they both looked at each other in dismay, thinking the house must be haunted after all.

"It's probably the mice, go and see."

"You go and see," replied the younger officer.

The older police officer cautiously opened the bedroom door to an earth-shattering, shrill shrieking sound, a snarl and a low eerie howling, then a loud hiss. He stepped back in shock!

"What is it?" the other policeman cried, stepping back in alarm at the evil noise coming from outside the door, his eyes wide open with fear.

"It's only the cat!" he told him, breathing a sigh of relief.

"I'll be glad when I'm out of here, it's a bit spooky here," the other replied.

They opened a door into a large en-suite bathroom decorated in white with gold coloured fittings.

The cold tap in the wash basin dripped loudly with an uncanny echoing sound.

They checked the other rooms; one of them was a dressing room with wardrobes around all the walls. They turned on their torches to investigate.

"Look here, inside this wardrobe!" one of them cried out. It was full of drawers and a large mirror. Each drawer was full of expensive jewellery – necklaces, earrings, bracelets, brooches, rings and tiaras.

"Where did she get all those? She wouldn't need them here surely." One wardrobe was full of expensive evening gowns and others had dresses and coats hung up in clothes covers. Another wardrobe had shoes of all different styles and colours, neatly placed on the shelves within. On top of the wardrobes were a lot of hat boxes and suitcases.

"Well, she hasn't taken her suitcases with her," one of the police officers remarked.

There was a dressing table stood in front of the window, with a set of silver backed brushes and combs, with a matching hand mirror. There were several wigs on stands and in the drawers were expensive looking lingerie. On the windowsill stood a pair of binoculars. The view from the window was overlooking the graveyard.

"I wonder what she was spying on from here?" the senior officer asked. The other officer shrugged his shoulders.

The other rooms were spare furnished bedrooms and a large family bathroom.

"You better check the airing cupboard; make sure her body isn't in there."

No body was found.

They climbed up a steep set of wooden stairs to the third floor and checked the two cold, dimly lit, long empty rooms with their torches. Cobwebs and dust were everywhere. The bare floorboards creaked and appeared to moan under their weight. A shudder ran down their spines.

"It doesn't look as if the cleaner ever comes up here!" remarked the older man.

"I don't blame her; I wouldn't like to come up here on my own either!"

"These rooms look like long dormitories, probably one for the boys and one for the girls. There are old fashioned locks on the doors, look, I bet they were locked in at night, no way of escaping if there was a fire! The staff probably had the luxury of the bedrooms on the second level." The wind rattled the small metal windows, and whistled eerily through the cracks.

"I'm out of here!" cried one of them.

"Me too!" shouted the other.

They were relieved to get outside. The locksmith got out of his car and secured the back door. The police officers checked the Range Rover and walked around the overgrown gardens to see if there was a fresh burial site. The cat was jumping through the long grass in front of them. They checked the greenhouse and garden shed which were both in disrepair – they had the usual garden equipment in them but no body was found.

"While we're here, I'll ask the glazier, Alan Grey, a few more questions."

Alan didn't answer his door at his cottage, so they knocked on a door of the row of cottages across the road.

"Do you know where we can find Alan Grey?" the policeman asked.

A teenage girl wearing a crop top, leggings and flip flops had answered the door. She folded her arms and leaned on the door frame. She replied, "He's out doing a job, I saw him from the school bus. He's at Joe Thur's place at the old forge."

The two policemen climbed into their car and drove down the village.

"I don't think the teenager knows it's February with what she was wearing!" one of them remarked, laughing.

"It's more of how they look these days with the younger ones, than keeping warm," came the reply.

They saw Alan standing high up on a ladder repairing a window.

"We have a few more questions to ask, if you don't mind."

"Give me a minute, I'm nearly done here." Alan descended the ladder and turned towards them.

"When you repaired the window for Mrs Hilda Redford-Hamilton did you actually see her that day?"

"Aye, I did, she rung me and asked me to go over there. She showed me the cracked window, I replaced it and she paid me cash."

"What date was this?"

"Now you're asking…as I said last time, I haven't a clue, I can only say about six months ago."

"Thank you again for your time," one of the policemen told him.

In the police car the two of them chatted.

"If Alan isn't lying then the thief, or the murderer, or both, had a key or was invited into Hilda's house."

"She could have committed suicide somewhere and has not been found," the younger officer suggested.

"I don't think she would leave her adored cat Winston behind," was the reply. "Her vehicle, money, credit cards, those valuable paintings, jewels and ornaments were not stolen, only the computer, box file and something out of the desk drawer as far as we know."

"Do you think she could have had something on someone and they killed her, took her house keys and accessed the house that way… or she could have let him in if she knew him and then he killed her; and he stole whatever she had on him?" asked the younger officer.

"Well we didn't see any keys in the front door or in her handbag and the door was locked, so you may be right there."

They left to go back to the police station to make a report. They had ruled out Hilda being on holiday, death by natural causes and suicide. She had possibly been kidnapped or murdered.

The forensic team arrived to carry out an extensive forensic investigation of The Old Vicarage and her vehicle; they collected any fingerprints, hair samples from Hilda's brushes, and a discarded paper tissue spotted with blood which was found in the wastepaper basket . They had found an air rifle behind one of the Christmas trees and pellets in a cupboard; they bagged them up for more forensic analysis.

The creaking floorboards near the desk had one of them curious. He lifted the large square green Persian rug in front of the desk and found the offending floorboards; he was able to lift them up as they weren't nailed down.

Underneath was a large black metal box. They lifted it out by its handles, but it was locked.

"The key is bound to be in this room somewhere, for convenience." They all began to search.

"It could be sellotaped under a drawer in the desk."

"I'll look around the fireplace," uttered another.

"How tall is she? She could have stood on a chair and slipped it onto the metal saucers holding the candle bulbs on the light fittings above."

"Try it," one remarked, placing a chair under the light fitting. "Found it!" The metal box was opened.

"Wow, this woman has been very busy – look at all these photos, copies of typed letters and tapes… There must be thousands of pounds here as well! What a treasure trove of information!" They all laughed; it was like finding pandora's box!

"If she took these explicit photos, where is her camera?" the police officer asked.

"Perhaps that was what was stolen out of the top drawer!"

SECRETS

The village hall was open that night – for 'pub night'. Volunteers manned the bar and young women collected the glasses from the tables and washed them. There was a loud hum of voices, nearly the whole village adult community was packed into the small stone-built hall. They'd all heard about the police investigation.

"Police were there this afternoon, they were in the house, I saw their torchlights and their cars outside," a gruff male voice shouted above the noise.

"I wonder what they were looking for?" asked another.

"Her dead body perhaps," retorted a young male.

A bearded man spoke up. "She's supposed to be on a long holiday, isn't she?"

"That's just rumours, I bet," replied another.

"Well, I won't miss her, I hated that evil woman," a disgruntled man uttered, venting his feelings.

"I don't think anyone liked her, she was full of her airs and graces and that posh voice, well I'm sure that was a put on," assumed an elderly woman.

"I wonder how she became so wealthy and why on earth would she want to come and live in Deadend village? She's obviously not a country type like us folk."

"Maybe she's running away from her past!" suggested a young male.

"Maybe her rich husband kicked her out!" laughed another.

"Murdered him more like!" an elderly woman replied. They all roared with laughter.

"She was a bit of a man hater, and do you remember Jack's dog being shot – it had an air rifle pellet in its back leg. She probably shot it for running in her posh garden."

"Her garden is no longer her pride and joy now, it's going to rack and ruin."

"Aye, do you remember Gail's cat dying – it was poisoned, so the vet said. She probably did that to stop it fouling her immaculate lawn."

"You're probably right, I'm glad she's gone and I hope she doesn't come back," another disgruntled person remarked.

****

At the police station they sifted through Mrs Hilda Redford-Hamilton's post and found the first letter she hadn't opened and read.

"Allowing for delivery after the letter was franked, it could have been 29th August 2018 when Hilda disappeared."

"Didn't Christine Holmes go missing on that date or around there?" asked one alert detective.

"Yes, I believe you're right! Why would two people go missing on the same day from the same village? One found in the lake and the other nowhere to be found?"

"Perhaps Christine Holmes saw something and drove off traumatized and that's how she ended up in the lake!"

"Or was she deliberately killed? We could have two homicides here. I want the church searched and especially the bell tower. Also, we'll set up house-to-house inquiries, I need a large map of the village and names of everyone living there. We need to know where everyone was around that date. Also, did anyone see Christine Holmes or her white car and who knows anything about Hilda Redford-Hamilton? Everyone is a suspect until they are eliminated from our inquiries."

"That's about 120 adults!" someone gasped.

"We need the list of services for the church and the event list for the village hall." The leading detective had pointed to key people to collect the information.

"We need a wide search of the surrounding area using cadaver dogs."

They sorted the photographs and the copies of letters taken from the metal box.

"It looks like she was blackmailing most of the villagers! She must have been spending her night times as a Peeping Tom!" one of the detectives exclaimed.

"There is plenty of motive for people to kill her and to steal her computer, camera, tape recorder and box file, to get rid of the evidence. They obviously didn't know about her second lot of copies under the floorboards."

"She certainly didn't need the blackmail money, so why did she go to this extreme?"

"Perhaps she was trying to clean up their immoral ways," remarked another, grinning.

"We'll have her bank account statements checked, see if she was short of income. She may look very wealthy from the outside, but she may have run out of a regular income."

****

Mrs Redford-Hamilton's cousin was informed that Hilda was still missing but the case was now being treated as a possible murder investigation, although they didn't have a body.

"I'll come over to England as soon as I can. I will probably be able to help with your inquiries," she told them.

The old church was searched; the young vicar was very helpful with their questions. He showed them to the bell tower through a doorway, they all ascended the old wooden steps to the first floor. Four bell ropes hung down from the belfry through small holes in the ceiling; they had blue and yellow woollen grips. They were told by the vicar that the grip was called a sally. The ropes were all tied onto hooks on the white painted walls which were discoloured with the damp. There were a few wooden chairs placed around the room and wooden boxes for the shorter bell ringers to stand on. In the corner stood a wooden chest. The detective opened it and found scrolls of paper.

"What are these?" he curiously asked.

"They're methods for ringing the bells," the vicar replied.

They inspected the ropes, furniture and the wooden floorboards mainly for skin tissue and blood stains but none were found. One of them ascended another flight of wooden steps and opened a wooden trap door to check the area around the four bells on the next level. He could see the four wheels attached to the bells and the ropes around the wheels. Nothing was found, only the sticks on the windowsill that the jackdaws had pushed through the wooden slatted windows.

They both followed the vicar down the steps into the nave of the church; each pew was scrutinized. The altar and around where the organist sat were also examined. The vestry and the other storerooms were searched. Nothing was found. They diligently searched the grounds and the church yard; there was nothing.

"We would like to interview you if it's convenient," the police officer asked the vicar.

"Of course, we'll go to The New Vicarage." The vicar led the way, they sat in the kitchen, and a pot of tea was made for them.

"What were you doing on Wednesday 29th August 2018?"

"I'll have to get my diary…Ah, yes, I was at the church most of the day, doing a few repairs and tidying up."

"Did you see anyone?"

"No, we don't have services on that day as there are various clubs going on at the village hall all day."

"What did you do in the evening?"

"I was here, writing a sermon."

"Can you hear the telephone from here?"

"Yes, I have a telephone in the hallway."

"We have a copy of a letter addressed to you; you are being blackmailed."

There was silence; the vicar looked stunned. The colour drained from his face.

"How did you receive the letter?" asked the detective.

"I found it under the vestry door. The church is never locked."

"Did you pay?"

"Yes, I did," the vicar replied.

"How did you pay?"

"I paid the £1000 in cash in a plastic bag, hidden at the back of the graveyard – as you'll have seen from the letter, I was given a specific time and date. I hid to see who was going to collect it. I left an hour later as no one had arrived. The next day the bag had gone."

The two police officers left and chatted in the car. They had remembered the binoculars in Hilda's dressing room which overlooked the graveyard. "She was obviously observing her victims to see if they had paid," remarked one of the officers.

"Why would the vicar say he saw no one on the day Christine Holmes disappeared? She was supposed to have visited the church's bell tower."

"Perhaps she never came here and set off home for some reason."

"Why would he say he was at The New Vicarage that night? Christine's sister was ringing him and he never answered. So, where was he? He didn't even ask us where we had found the copy of the blackmailer's letter!"

"He looks like our prime suspect, the blackmailer was threatening to expose him, he had a lot to lose."

The house-to-house inquiries began in earnest. A police officer knocked on the spritely eighty-year old's red front door.

"Come in, I'll make you a nice cup of tea for you both," offered the kind, cheerful woman. There was a lovely smell of apple pies baking in the oven.

"No thank you, not now, we are here to ask you a few questions about Mrs Hilda Redford-Hamilton. When did you last see her?"

"Well now, let me think a minute, it must be about six months ago. My son was staying with me as he was mending my guttering for me. He told me he heard her shouting and screaming at something in her garden, but he couldn't see what it was." She thought for a while. "She didn't turn up for the AGM at the village hall on 1st September and she was on the committee. She didn't even give her apologies!"

"Did she have any visitors?" asked the police officer.

"We had meetings in her dining room occasionally, we thought they should be in The New Vicarage like we always did. She said there wasn't enough space around the table and insisted on having the meetings at her house. No, I didn't see any outsiders going to her house to visit."

"You have said she kept herself to herself the last time we met, yet you now say she was on the committee and had meetings in her house."

"Well, I meant she kept her past to herself; no one knew where she had come from and why she came to live in the village, she is quite a mystery. She never went to the pub nights and everyone goes there."

"Did you see a white Vauxhall Corsa or a middle-aged woman by the church or in the village on 29th August 2018?"

"No, I can't say I did. She would have stuck out like a sore thumb if she was a stranger, villagers all know everyone around here."

The next terraced house was Gail's home. It was brightly painted in the sitting room where they were invited into, to sit.

"I'm sure she poisoned my poor cat, Ellie. If it wasn't for the vet, Ellie would have died. I have no time for that woman."

"When did you last see her?"

"Err... the 2nd August, last year. I went round to give her a piece of my mind, that was the day Ellie was poisoned. I was distraught and very angry!"

"What did she say?"

"She denied it of course, in her brazen haughty manner she told me to get off her property and never come back!" The police officer asked about the stranger in the village but Gail knew nothing about it.

Wendy Stubbs lived next door in the same terrace.

"We don't mingle in the same circles, I'm a teacher at the village school, so my time after school is mainly with the brownies, sports club and crafts with the little ones. I never see much of Mrs Redford-Hamilton."

"We have found a copy of a letter addressed to you – you are being blackmailed."

Wendy gasped. "Wherever did you find that?"

"It's not important. Please answer the question."

Wendy looked pale and shaken.

"Yes – he, well I'm assuming it's a he, wanted £1000 or he would tell my husband and the education authorities about my affair. I paid, of course, to stop any scandal. We would not have been welcome in the village, if that got out."

"Where were the photos taken of you and Craig Ruddy in a compromising position?"

"At his place. Whoever it was must have been spying on us at his house, late at night and took the photos of us in his lounge; we had the patio doors open. Please don't mention anything to my husband, it's all finished, it was just a fling."

"Who was blackmailing you?"

"I've no idea!"

"How did you receive the letter?"

"It was hand delivered through my letterbox, it must have been in the middle of the night as it wasn't there last thing. I found it the following morning."

"How did you pay the money?"

"It was in cash, I had to hide it behind a very old gravestone at the back of the graveyard near the bushes; it was on a specific date and time."

"Do you know where Hilda Redford-Hamilton is?"

"I have no idea and quite frankly, I don't care!"

They asked her about the stranger.

"Come to think about it, I did see a white car on the grass verge by the church. I don't know which date or time it was, but it was definitely an outsider – villagers all know not to park on the verges on the single-track road. Whoever it was should have parked at the village hall car park."

The police officers moved on to Bill Dobson's detached house – he was the organist and worked as a music teacher at the secondary school in the town.

"I was away on holiday at the end of August until 4th September – I went to visit family. I saw Hilda at the church services and about the village. I didn't really have much to do with her," he told them.

"We have a copy of a letter addressed to you, blackmailing you. You were having a homosexual relationship with the vicar according to the letter."

"Oh no, this will ruin us if it got out!" Bill cried out, physically shaking, his hands held up to his pale face.

"Did you pay the money?"

"Yes, of course I paid, it was £1000, what else could I do?"

"How did you pay?"

"I had to leave it behind a certain gravestone in the graveyard at a certain time."

"Did you see who retrieved it?"

"No." He didn't know anything about the stranger or about Mrs Redford-Hamilton's whereabouts.

Jim Oak was next to be interviewed. He lived in a small detached house.

"I mend shoes, I'm semi-retired now, still enjoying my work at 79!" he told them with a pleasant smile.

"Your place is appropriately named, cobbler's cottage," smiled the police officer.

"Aye, I renamed it!" He was sat in a rocking chair, happily smoking his pipe.

"When did you last see Mrs Redford-Hamilton?"

"I returned some repaired shoes on the 29th August about 9.30 in the morning, last year. It was my wife's birthday; sadly, she's passed away since, shortly after, it was."

"I'm sorry to hear that. Did you actually speak to Mrs Redford-Hamilton?"

"Aye I did, she was complaining about the jackdaws poking sticks through the wooden slats in the belfry, in the church tower. She's one of our bell ringers, in fact she's the master bell ringer."

"What sort of a person is she?"

Jim laughed. "She is full of her own importance, but she was alright with me, she always paid me and tipped me well."

"What are all the white boxes near everyone's homes, with names on?" queried one of the officers.

Jim chuckled and took out his pipe from his mouth.

"Well, if you have anything to sell, you leave it in the white box marked with your name. If you – the buyer – have apples from your orchard say, you just swap it or leave some money. There's eggs, fruit and vegetables of all kinds, baking, craft things, clothes – you name it, you can generally get it somewhere! People advertise what they have in the village hall with a suggested price. We don't have a shop, see, so we manage the best we can. It's all done on honesty. We can buy fresh bread from Sam up the village, lovely apple pies from Mildred at the red door…"

The policeman smiled and interrupted. "You're well organized as a community, I'm impressed."

"Who lives next door?" asked the other policeman.

"A young couple, they've a springer spaniel, it was shot with an air rifle in its back leg, last year. They blamed Mrs H.R.H. at The Old Vicarage."

"We'll ask them about it another day, we are heading back to the police station. Thank you for your help. Oh, did you see a stranger in the village with a white car on 29th August 2018? I nearly forgot to ask."

"No, I didn't," came the reply.

The policemen drove away in their car laughing. "The inland revenue, health and safety and the food standards agency would have a field day here, if they knew what was going on!"

"At least we know Hilda was alive and well on the morning of 29th August 2018."

"Double check the day out on the calendar on your mobile phone."

"It was definitely Wednesday," replied the other officer. "We also know the white car was seen at sometime on the grass verge, outside the church."

"Christine Holmes' sister said it was 29th August 2018 when Christine visited the bell tower. It's unusual for two people to go missing from a remote village and one to be found in the lake."

****

Hilda Redford-Hamilton's cousin arrived from Canada; she was staying in the nearby town. She arrived at the police station as soon as she could. She introduced herself as Ann Harrison. "I can give you the full background on my cousin as we were brought up together."

"It would be very useful as no one in the village appears to know anything about her," the detective replied.

Ann was offered a seat.

"Hilda was orphaned at three years old – her parents died in a train crash. My mother and father took her in and raised her." She got out a copy of Hilda's birth certificate from her handbag.

"Hilda Smith, born 20th August 1949," read the police officer. Ann also handed him a photo of her.

"It was taken about a year ago – she is a beautiful woman, don't you think?"

A tray with cups of tea and biscuits were brought into the interview room at that moment. Ann took a sip from her cup.

"I was five years older than Hilda; she was a real handful; I think my mother regretted taking her in. Tantrums! You have never seen anything like it!" Ann laughed and picked up a biscuit.

"She liked to control everyone, she was cruel too, with animals that is, she had no empathy at all. She would steal my father's air rifle and shoot sparrows on the lawn and cats if she could get them! The little devil even cut off the tails of all the kittens my cat had!"

The police officer looked astounded, remembering Jack's springer spaniel was shot in the leg with an air rifle.

"When she became a teenager, she was out of control and was very flirty; she had a good figure and was like a film star with her looks. She was tall with dark brown hair, she attracted older men – boys of her own age couldn't handle her!"

"Where were you brought up?" asked the police officer, curious to find out more.

"Manchester. She became a secretary, eventually she worked for a big corporation... the name has slipped from my mind just now – old age creeping in, I'm afraid! Well, the next thing we knew she was 'head over heels in love' with the owner, Ron Dudley-Fairfax – he was old enough to be her father! At 22 years of age she married him, he was 51!"

The police officers could see where her money was coming from. Ann took another sip of tea.

"She stopped work as soon as she was married; he was a multimillionaire! He adored her, he worshiped the ground she walked on, she was like a trophy on his arm to him. He loved to show her off. He bought her loads of expensive clothes and jewellery, she had piano lessons, singing lessons, elocution lessons, private dance classes and cordon bleu cookery classes – to teach her to become a high society lady. They attended London balls and mixed with the aristocracy!"

"So, what happened to her husband?"

"About 10 years after their wedding he died – he fell down the stairs and broke his neck! She pretended she was distraught but I knew her too well, it was all crocodile tears. She had only married him for his money, she didn't love him."

"Did they have any children?"

"Yes, they had a daughter, they named her Elizabeth Charlotte Dudley-Fairfax. Hilda would have been 24 years old when she was born. The poor girl lost the father she absolutely adored, she was only eight at the time, it must have been devastating for her. Hilda packed her off to boarding school, poor child. Hilda hated children, her own and everyone else's."

"Who was the beneficiary of his will?"

"It all went to Hilda; he was besotted with her."

"What about his daughter?"

"Hilda had convinced him she would take care of her. He believed her."

"So, when did she remarry?" the detective asked.

"She started dating straight away, no shame in her. She married three years later to an even richer man this time, Charles Redford-Hamilton. He was 73 and she was only 35!"

"How and when did he die?"

"He died about three years later, they were out walking and he fell down a slope, hitting his head on a rock! Of course, she got his millions as well."

"So, what happened to the daughter?"

"When Elizabeth turned 16, she left home, never to be seen again. She absolutely hated her mother, they used to argue all the time. Elizabeth wrote to me and told me, that if she didn't put her clothes in her wardrobe properly, she was severely reprimanded. She wasn't allowed out with boys or her friends unless accompanied by her mother. Hilda was very controlling with her; it must have been suffocating for poor Elizabeth. Hilda thought her daughter was very weak and didn't want her led astray – it would have wrecked Hilda's reputation!"

"So, you have no idea where Elizabeth is?"

"No, she probably didn't keep in touch with me for fear I may one day accidently mention her to Hilda or where she lived." Ann finished her biscuit and cup of tea.

The police officer replied, "It sounds suspicious to me the way her rich husbands died and the disappearance of her daughter."

"You're not the only one. She was nicknamed 'the black widow'. People in high places did inform the police about the fact, two husbands had died in her presence but there was no evidence of foul play, that they could see. She was snubbed in high society and her social circles until eventually no one wanted to know her. She frittered her money away on failed business projects and investments – half of it had already disappeared in the stock market crash of 1987. She started going on lots of expensive cruises and her waistline expanded. She had expensive plastic surgery, tummy tucks and breast implants trying to keep her figure and her looks; she was hoping to find another rich husband. She was getting older and none of the wealthy men found her appealing anymore. That's when she decided to move to Deadend village to start a new life. I've never been there but from the photos she sent me it looks as if she was playing the part of 'the lady of the manor', buying a house that size. I believe she had a cleaner and a gardener."

"Yes, she did, she didn't tell either one of them she was going away. What a life she has had. Do you think she became depressed at her 'fall from grace' and took her own life somewhere?" the detective asked.

"Hilda! No, definitely not, if she hasn't died of natural causes then someone has murdered her!"

"She could have been kidnapped?" the other detective suggested.

"Not very likely, there has been no ransom demand, has there? Can you imagine kidnapping an arrogant, haughty woman like her! They would never have managed to contain her; they would have been driven around the bend and murdered her for a bit of peace and quiet!" She laughed out loud.

"You don't appear to like her very much. Why have you remained in touch all these years?"

"It's a promise I made to my dear mother on her deathbed. My mother begged me to look after Hilda. Mother died of cancer when Hilda was 14 years old. I was just married by then – you can imagine it was a nightmare. Hilda managed to split up my husband and I. She left home at 15 and trained as a secretary. My husband and I managed to get back together and we moved to Canada out of the way! I kept in touch with Hilda by letters and cards to keep my promise to Mother. I sent her money at first to keep her going during her training. As you can see Hilda was quite good at looking after herself!"

"Do you know who the beneficiaries are to her will?"

Ann looked surprised. "I hadn't thought about her will – didn't you find it when you searched the house?"

"No, we didn't find anything like that," the detective replied.

"Well that's strange, she will have one somewhere. Perhaps whoever are the beneficiaries, they could have killed her to inherit her money!"

"It had crossed our minds," the detective uttered, smiling at her. "Well, thank you for coming all this way, you have given us a lot of background on Hilda. I must warn you, if you are going to The Old Vicarage some of the rooms are a mess downstairs due to mice infestation."

"I thought I may as well take a look as I'm here, I know where she has hidden the spare key – she told me in a letter, in case I needed it for an emergency. Well, I definitely think this is an emergency! My husband and I will be going there tomorrow afternoon, if that is alright?" Ann asked him.

"Yes, that's fine, we will have completed our search by then and forensics have already been through," the detective informed her. "If you have anything else that would help with our enquiries, please let us know."

Ann added, "I'm here with my husband for a few days, we are staying at 'The Duke' Hotel in the town, in case you need to contact me."

When she had left, one of the detectives suggested, "We should try and find out where the daughter is – she can't have just disappeared, unless she was murdered. If she is alive and well, she could be the beneficiary to Hilda's will and could be the murderer?"

The wide search of the land around the village using the cadaver dogs had come to an end.

None of the villagers were interested in volunteering to help in the search. The trained dogs had quickly walked through the terrain, held on leads by their handlers. They sniffed the grass and stones as they went along but there were no signals from the dogs indicating they had found anything.

The media had been informed about the missing woman. Her photograph with a description was displayed on the TV and on the front page of the local and national newspapers; appealing for information of her whereabouts. Reporters had started to arrive at the village interested in interviewing the locals, but most of the villagers shunned them; they hated their privacy being invaded.

THE WILL

The police continued with their house-to-house enquiries. They arrived at 3 Fell Houses, a detached house with brightly painted garden ornaments scattered about the garden. There was a dog bowl and a chewed-up ball by the door; in the hallway stood a baby buggy.

They asked the young couple, Jack and Suzy, "When did you last see Hilda Redford-Hamilton?" Suzy retrieved her diary from upstairs. The spaniel approached the police officers, very excited; he was furiously wagging his tail. Jack grabbed his collar to stop him jumping up at them. Suzy entered the light airy room with her small diary in her hand; she shuffled through the pages.

"Possibly around the 28th August last year. I was going for a dental appointment, she pulled out of her drive right in front of me, she wasn't even looking for traffic or anyone! We nearly crashed; I had a baby on board!" Suzy informed them.

The police officer asked Jack, "What about you?" Jack stroked his beard in deep thought.

"I haven't a clue when I saw her last, she never comes to the pub nights, that's beneath her, I think. You've likely heard about our dog being shot; we suspect it could have been her. No one else in the village would do such a thing."

They hadn't seen the stranger in the village so the police officers moved on to the next terrace to speak to a bachelor, Callum Peach. He looked to be in his thirties, he had blue eyes quite close together, which gave him a very distinctive face. He couldn't remember the last time he saw Mrs Redford-Hamilton either.

"We have a copy of a blackmailer's letter addressed to you."

Callum was speechless for a moment.

"Where did you get that?" he cried out, extremely annoyed.

The police officer ignored his question and asked, "Did you pay this £1000 demand?"

"Yes, I did. Gill got one as well, we didn't want it broadcasted out into the community, we would have been vilified. I delivered the £1000 to the gravestone as directed."

"How was the letter sent?" Callum was asked.

"It was in my white box outside, where I sell my small pottery pieces, it was there first thing in the morning. I admit I was horrified, I had no idea who was lurking around taking photographs of our affair. Gill's married to David Lacey, they have a lot of problems." Callum hadn't seen the stranger or the white car.

They moved on to the house next door in the same terrace, but they were out. The end house was Alan's, the glazier; they had already questioned him apart from asking him about the white car. They arrived at a detached house called the 'Paddocks'. Daniel Brown, a joiner and builder, answered the door. He was still in his overalls and had sawdust in his hair.

The same questions were repeated by the police.

"No idea when I last saw her, it would have been last year sometime. I heard she went away on a long holiday. I've seen her walking about the village late at night, weird woman. I never saw a white car or a stranger – did you, Kate?"

Kate Brown, who was a solicitor's secretary, began to speak. "No, it's next door you should investigate. She's 16 now but someone made her pregnant at 15! That's under-age sex!"

"Do you know who he was?"

"I've a good idea – she hung around the farrier, Steve Mann, helping with shoeing horses. He disappeared quite suddenly when she was about two months pregnant."

"How old was he and where did he live in the village?" the police officer asked.

"He'd be in his forties, he rented the last terrace house on Fell Face, he stored all his shoeing equipment in a double horse trailer and drove it all over the place with his Land Rover to his customers. The girl, Carla Robinson, often went with him at weekends."

The police officers left and walked to the following detached house; it also had a paddock with an Arab pony grazing there. No one answered the door.

"It looks like Hilda Redford-Hamilton missed this scandal about the girl – we haven't any copies of blackmailing letters to the farrier."

"I thought this village had a zero-crime rate but it's a den of iniquity! Blackmailing, under-age sex and possibly murder and now another person is missing!"

"We will have to report back and see if the farrier, Steve Mann, can be found."

Two other police officers had contacted Hilda Redford-Hamilton's cleaner, Lotty Sanders, to meet at The Old Vicarage that day. They wanted her to walk through the house and tell them what had been taken.

They entered the hallway through the arched front door. The locksmith was there, the police officers had a court order to show him that they had permission to enter the premises as before.

"Is there a coat missing from the coat hooks?" one of them asked Lotty.

"No," she replied, glancing that way.

"I suppose it was summer when she left so she probably didn't need a coat. Did she have a mobile phone?" the police officer asked.

"Yes, she carried it around in her pocket. She wore wool jackets or in the summer she wore dresses and cardigans with pockets. She told me she generally had her mobile phone turned off, she hated being interrupted. She said 'it was for her convenience not for everyone else's convenience'. I didn't blame her." They entered the dining room. Lotty looked shocked at the amount of dust on the table and the other surfaces.

"Is anything missing from this room?"

"Yes, a red carpet about two metres square."

Both the police officers were thinking the carpet had been used to roll Hilda's body in, to transport it to another place. Lotty checked the dresser but couldn't see any of the silver cutlery or the crockery were missing. None of the silver peacock ornaments or the silver platters adorning the dresser had been removed. They carried on through to the drawing room. Lotty gasped at the long black cobweb hanging from the paintings.

"Nothing is missing that I can see," she told them, closing the piano fallboard to protect the keys. They walked across the large hallway into the lounge.

"Nothing missing here," Lotty informed them. They walked through into the office.

Lotty gasped. "Her computer is missing!"

"What did she keep in the top drawer?" the police officer asked.

"She usually kept it locked so I don't know, perhaps she kept her expensive camera in there... Oh, look, a box file is missing!"

"What was in it, do you know?"

"No, she was always with me in the same room when I was cleaning, probably to make sure I wasn't noseying around. I never saw what was in anything in here."

"Did she ever mention a will?"

"No, she told me nothing, I'm just the cleaner!"

"Did she ever speak about a daughter?"

Lotty looked stunned. "Did she have a daughter? She didn't tell me anything!"

"The last day you cleaned here, did she seem alright to you?"

"Yes, it was just a normal day, it was a Wednesday."

"How did you find out she wasn't here?"

"I came to work the following morning, I can't remember the date, it was at 10 as usual, my shift was 10 till 12. I knocked on the door but there was no reply, I knocked a few times but no answer. I even went around to the back door but no one appeared to be about. I checked the garden, greenhouse and shed but she wasn't there! I even phoned her landline on my mobile but no reply. So, I went to see the vicar to see if he knew anything. He thought she may have gone on holiday and not told anyone."

"Did she normally not tell anyone when she went away?"

"I've only worked for her for a little while, and in that time, she didn't go away on holiday," came the reply.

They walked around the rest of the house, Lotty was distressed at the state of the kitchen and the pantry. Nothing more had been taken as far as she knew; she didn't know about the dressing room, she told them she had been forbidden to enter that room and also the attic. The police officers asked her about the stranger and the white car but she knew nothing about them.

"Where are all the cleaning things and vacuum cleaner and things like that?" asked one of the officers – he hadn't noticed them during the search.

"I'll show you." Lotty walked into the inner hallway and slid open a panel, inside were shelves with cleaning products neatly placed in a row; there were brooms, pans and brushes, several vacuum cleaners, mops and buckets.

"A secret room – neat!" the young police officer was impressed. "Are there anymore secret rooms?"

"Not that I know of," replied Lotty.

"Who worked for Mrs Redford-Hilton before you?"

"Old Mrs Ackroyd, the local gossip, she was sacked as she was caught rummaging around in the office. It's probably why I was never left on my own. Mrs Redford-Hamilton was a very private person."

When the police officers left they discussed the visit and decided to report back to base and arrange for forensics to come and investigate the broom cupboard – it may have been the place where the body was hidden and stored for a while.

****

The following day, Ann and her husband Edward arrived in a rented car at The Old Vicarage. They were surprised, the place looked even bigger than the photos of the house had suggested.

"We need to go around the back, five strides from the back door there will be a stone or something, the spare key should be under that – she had once told me that in a letter," Ann informed her husband, Edward. The pathway was overgrown with weeds and moss. They saw the garden was in a mess, weeds had taken over and the lawn was overgrown.

"Here it is," Edward shouted, as he turned over a large stone garden statue of a cat and had found the spare key.

They walked around to the arched front door and turned the old rusty iron key in the heavy ornate metal lock, to let themselves in. They walked into the large hallway and opened the glass door into the dining room to their right. They noticed the image of the vicarage was etched into the glass, the same across the hallway in another glass door. They marvelled at the splendour of the long table and the splendid light fitting above it.

"It could do with a thorough cleaning in here," Ann remarked. "Oh, look at these wonderful peacocks, she certainly had good taste!" She parted the dresser's dark wood doors to see inside. "I wonder if she invited any of the villagers for dinner parties?"

"I doubt it, she would think they were well beneath her," Edward responded.

Ann opened the drawers. "Look at these." She began lifting out a silver fork. "The cutlery is solid silver!"

"Well she wouldn't bother with silver plated now, would she!" her husband replied. He walked over to the fireplace to admire the regal female in the painting, hung above the marble mantelpiece.

"Who is this beautiful lady in a tiara?"

"The lady, my dear, is Hilda Jane Redford-Hamilton, my cousin!"

"She's come a long way from being Hilda Smith!" he replied. They carried on into the drawing room.

"These paintings must be worth a fortune and look at that grand piano!" Ann declared, mesmerized with the opulence of her surroundings. "She lived like royalty! We need to find her office, her will will be there; it may give us a clue who the murderer is," Ann told her husband, in an excited voice.

They crossed the hall, opening the glass door into the large lounge, and she scanned the lavish Victorian styled room and admired the splendid fireplace. She opened the door on the back wall.

"Ah, this is it! Yes, just as I thought – she still has our grandfather's desk bureau in the corner there... Just watch this." She slid out a secret panel by pressing a button underneath. There sat a brown envelope addressed to her cousin from her solicitor.

"She would know I would remember this secret compartment, we used to play with it when we were children, when Grandfather was out. This must be it! I wonder who the beneficiaries are?" She took out the will from the envelope and began to read the contents out aloud.

"'This is the last Will and Testament of Hilda Jane Redford-Hamilton of The Old Vicarage, Deadend village'... etcetera, etcetera... 'I hereby revoke all former wills' etcetera.... 'I appoint the partners at the time of my death in the firm of'...such and such...Ah here it is... 'I bequeath all of my estate'... that's not want I want." She skimmed through hurriedly wanting to know the beneficiaries... "'My residuary estate'... Wow, I'm getting it all after expenses! I'm even the executor of her will!" She gasped and sat down on the swivel desk chair by the other desk, reading it over and over again. Edward put on his reading glasses, he peered over her shoulder to read it to make sure she had understood it correctly.

"Oh, my gosh! She's left it all to me! I'll be the prime suspect now she's been murdered!" Ann cried out, doubly shocked.

"We don't know she has been murdered, do we?" he cried out in dismay.

"What else could have happened? She wouldn't have gone anywhere without Winston!"

"The police should have a copy of this," Edward declared.

"What! Give them evidence against me, not on your Nelly!" Ann replied in dismay.

Her husband grunted with annoyance.

"I'll make a copy of it on this old photocopier and put the original back where we found it," Ann retorted.

"What's the date on the will?"

"28th June 2017, it must have been done shortly after she moved here," Ann suggested.

They walked past the stairway into the inner hallway. They found the linen cupboard and the pantry to their right.

"Oh, my gosh! I'll have to tidy up this awful stinking mess in here, we will have to stay longer in England and let Len and Amy know, they can keep an eye on our place until we return to Canada."

"The garden needs a lot of work too," Edward muttered.

"We should ask the gardener and cleaner to come back and help us," Ann replied. They peeped into the small room with the toilet and wash basin.

"She can make even the smallest room look amazing!" Ann exclaimed.

They turned left into the kitchen.

"Oh no!" they both exclaimed in unison after seeing the fridge.

"What a mess! I wouldn't know where to begin!" Ann cried out, disappointed at the amount of work to do. They hurried into the utility room.

Ann opened the wardrobe freezer; each drawer was neatly labelled.

"No doubt she's used to cordon bleu cooking, not like us and our pizzas and fish 'n' chips!" They both laughed. They went into the boot room and saw her flowered patterned boots and the herbs.

"Oh, she still dried herbs like we did at home, in our humble beginnings. I wonder if she is a bell ringer too, like we were when we were young?"

Her husband opened the wooden shutters. On the small window ledge, outside, sat a black cat, which jumped off in fright when he saw them.

Ann declared, "That must be Winston, poor cat. We'll have to stay to look after him."

"I've found the key to the back door, it's on this hook, look," her husband remarked. The door creaked on its hinges as he opened it. Winston ran in, pleased to be home. He brushed against Ann's trouser legs. She picked him up and sat down on the stone slab and stroked him.

"He's looking well, someone must be feeding him," she uttered. She put him down and they walked back into the main hallway; the cat followed them. They all ascended the sweeping wide stairway with banister rails at each side.

"It reminds me of the staircase in the film 'Gone with the Wind'," Ann said, laughing. They stepped onto the gallery styled landing, and peeped over to admire the stairs from above. The spindled dark oak banisters were impressive, the plush red and gold Axminster carpet had brass stair rods on every stair.

Sunlight shone down in rays from a beautiful stained-glass dome in the ceiling above.

"She must have spent a fortune decorating and carpeting this place, it's like a palace!" Ann announced excitedly.

"Well, she had the money, what else could she do with it?" Edward replied sullenly.

They found Hilda's bedroom. They marvelled at the imposing four-poster bed with the blue drapes tied back with gold coloured rope tassels. The cover on the double bed matched the drapes. They saw her summer clothes and handbag neatly arranged on her bed.

Ann touched the white silk dressing gown draped over the blue and gold chaise longue, which was standing at the foot of the bed. She was very envious of what her cousin had. Stood in the corner was a Queen Anne style wardrobe in white and gold and a matching fitted carpet.

"We could move in, once we have tidied it all up!" Ann enthusiastically declared.

"I don't think that would be a very good idea, the police haven't found a body and they haven't found that will. We could pay the staff to keep it clean and tidy till we know the outcome."

They peeped into the en-suite bathroom.

"It's so beautiful, I'd love an en-suite bathroom like this," wished Ann.

Each wardrobe in the dressing room was opened one by one; Ann squealed in delight at the expensive items, particularly the jewellery. She tried on a diamond studded bracelet, lovingly admiring it. She lifted two white pearl stud earrings to her ears and gazed into the mirror. She was no beauty: her face was wrinkled with age, her bifocals didn't even make her look important. Her wavy grey hair was brushed back off the sides of her face.

"Mmm," she sighed at her reflection in the mirror.

"Your beautiful to me, dear, you don't need all these trappings, I like you just as you are."

She smiled at her loving husband's endearments.

"There must be a million pounds worth of jewellery in here!" Ann exclaimed, her eyes sparkling with elation again.

"She has no real security here, it must be a low crime area," Edward stated in amazement.

"We can't leave all this here – it will be stolen!" Ann exclaimed, turning to Edward.

"It's not ours to take, not yet anyway," Edward replied.

"What should we do?"

"We could hide it all somewhere in the house and inform the police so they know it hasn't been stolen," her concerned husband suggested.

"I think we should stay here; we can buy food in until I sort out the kitchen and pantry. It all needs protecting!"

They looked into the other bedrooms and entered the bathroom.

"Wow, this is a gorgeous bathroom too, she certainly knew how to lavishly decorate and furnish a place."

"She probably got all her ideas from mansions she had visited, going to parties at her husband's wealthy friends' places," Edward assumed.

They ascended the steep, old wooden stairs onto the third level; Winston scampered up after them. The tired old wooden door groaned and creaked when they opened it. The two long rooms had small fireplaces in the middle of the inner walls.

"What would these rooms be used for?" asked Ann, scanning the rooms.

"Probably for servants when it was first built; they needed a lot of labour in those days as water would have to be fetched in, washing was done by hand and then all the cleaning and meals to make. They would grow their own food and have livestock butchered. There were all the fires to make, no central heating and double glazing in those days!"

"It's bitterly cold up here, let's go downstairs and gets some heating on." Later they returned to their hotel in the town to retrieve their luggage and pay. They returned and slept in Hilda's bedroom that night. Winston was happy to snuggle up in his favourite place on the chaise longue.

The following day they managed to locate Lotty and Fred, who both agreed to come back to work. Ann helped Lotty in the house while her husband, Edward, helped Fred with the garden and repairs to the greenhouse and shed.

Lotty appeared to be quite shy with Ann, she didn't open up to her about herself, but Ann liked her all the same.

****

At the police station they were having a meeting and discussing what information and evidence they had. There was a large white board in front of the spacious room showing all the names and information that had been collected. The leading detective began, "We believe it is possible that Hilda's body may be wrapped in a large red rug carpet. All fly-tipping sites must be investigated, rubbish dumps and waste ground, although it's possible she may have been buried elsewhere."

"It must be remote, it's been six months now, someone would have found her by now," added an officer at the back of the room. "Forensics didn't find any evidence in the broom cupboard to suggest a body had been stored there."

"No will was found, so we don't know who the beneficiaries are – they could have killed her to inherit her wealth."

"I'm on trying to trace her daughter, I believe she changed her name by deed poll, she could have got married as well and may even be living abroad. I'll continue the search tomorrow," an officer updated them.

"How did you come on with the search for the farrier, Steve Mann?" asked the leading detective, looking towards another officer.

"He lives in Cornwall, I have his address here." He passed the sheet of paper over to the detective.

"I'll arrange for the local police to interview him," the lead detective informed the meeting.

"It appears the stranger's white car was seen parked on the grass verge outside the church. The vicar should be questioned again about this," another officer suggested. "At the same time, I'll ask him to corroborate Lotty's story about seeing the vicar when Hilda disappeared. It looks like he started the rumour about Hilda going on holiday."

The lead detective concluded from all the information that had been collected so far that Hilda was alive and well at about 9.30 am on the 29th of August 2018. At that time, she received her repaired shoes and through to 10 am to 12 pm when Lotty was cleaning for her. Christine Holmes was estimated to be there at the church around 2.30 pm on the same day in her white car. The search for Hilda, her daughter and the arrangements for an interview with the farrier would continue the following day.

"Now we come to the list of suspects! The top of the list is the vicar having a homosexual relationship with the organist Bill Dobson. They had a lot to lose if exposed. Wendy Stubbs, the teacher and married lover Craig Ruddy, the artist.

Then there's Callum Peach, the potter with married lover Gillian Lacey, a weaver.

We still have to interview about the blackmailing of married John Milton, a solicitor and his married lover Kate Brown, his secretary.

All this list of people have been blackmailed by Hilda Redford-Hamilton so anyone of them have a motive to kill her." He looked at the board and continued. "There is of course Steve Mann, the farrier, having underage sex with Carla Robinson – she is about six months pregnant. Steve Mann disappeared about two months into her pregnancy, probably when he found out about her condition.

As you say, he's living in Cornwall, we'll wait for the local police there to interview him about it and also if he knows anything about Hilda Redford-Hamilton's disappearance and Christine Holmes' visit to the church.

Run a check on all these suspects see if any of them have a criminal record," he ordered, pointing to an officer on the front row.

The following day, a police detective questioned the vicar at The New Vicarage.

"We have a witness who has come forward saying they saw a stranger's white car parked on the grass verge near the church; it would have belonged to Christine Holmes. Are you certain you didn't see anyone on 29th August 2018?"

"It's possible I may have slipped back to the vicarage to relieve myself and have a cup of tea, I can't just remember, I usually have a drink about 3 pm, she may have gone into the church then. I didn't see anyone."

"We estimate the middle-aged woman, Christine Holmes, would have arrived at the church at 2.30 pm."

"I'm sorry I can't help you. I didn't see anyone," the vicar repeated.

"Did anyone come to see you the following day?" the police officer asked.

"I can't remember," the vicar replied.

"Lotty said she came to see you, what was that about?" the detective asked.

"Oh, yes I remember, she was looking for Mrs Redford-Hamilton, I said she may have gone on holiday."

ANOTHER VICTIM

The house-to-house inquiries continued.

"I'm so pleased you are here!" exclaimed a distraught white-haired woman. "I'm Irene and here is my mother Kitty," she explained leading them into a small sitting room. Kitty looked very old and had a vacant stare. She was wrapped in a coloured blanket, rocking backwards and forwards in an old armchair.

"You are the first to be pleased to see us, is there anything wrong?" asked the police officer in a kind voice.

"I've been going through my mother's paperwork this morning and I came across her will. It's either forged or my mother signed it without knowing what she was doing."

"Who is the beneficiary of the will?" asked the senior officer.

"Mrs Hilda Redford-Hamilton!" replied the distraught daughter. "My mother always wanted me to be the sole beneficiary; I have no siblings. As you can see my mother suffers from dementia."

"What date is written on the will?"

"26th August 2018," replied Irene.

"That was three days before Mrs Redford-Hamilton disappeared," the police officer remarked.

"My mother was ill for a time in August – vomiting, tiredness and slurred speech. Do you think Hilda was trying to poison her and trying to get her property and money?

Hilda always called every day to see my mother and bought her gifts of food! I don't think she knew who I was, as my mother would not have mentioned me, due to her memory loss. I always called my mother Kitty – Hilda may have thought I was just the carer."

"Do you have any food stored in the deep freeze that Mrs Redford-Hamilton gifted?"

"I'll have a look." Irene disappeared out of the room.

Out of earshot the police officer uttered:

"Blackmail, shooting a dog, poisoning a cat and now possible attempted murder and fraud – is there nothing this evil woman isn't capable of?" The police officer shook his head in disbelief.

Irene returned carrying a small carton of cherry mousse. "I don't know if this was anything to do with Hilda, it's not something I would buy, my mother and I don't like cherries."

"If you don't mind, we'll take it for forensic analysis. I will arrange for your mother to have toxicology blood and urine tests."

"Do you have a previous will?" the younger female officer asked.

"Well yes, a copy will still be lodged at our solicitor's, she drew up the will," Irene replied.

"Have a word with your solicitor and ask her to send us a copy to compare it with this one. We will take this latest will as evidence of a possible fraud. When did you last see Hilda Redford-Hamilton?"

"I really can't remember; I live next door to Kitty and pop in frequently throughout the day; it was a long time ago that I last saw Hilda here."

"Did you see a stranger or a white car parked by the church on 29th August 2018?"

"No, I'm not down at that end of the village much."

The police left with the evidence and handed it to another police officer to return it immediately to their headquarters in the town.

The police officers decided to question the pregnant girl. They drove back down the quiet village road. It was very cold but no longer windy.

Carla Robinson was in the paddock grooming her Arab pony. The pony's rope halter was tied to a metal ring on the outside of the wooden stable, its blue stable rug was slung over the half door. Carla was small for her age with beautiful long, auburn, curly hair flowing from underneath her knitted pom-pom hat. The policewoman approached her while the other police officer knocked on the front door of the house.

"Hi, I'm Amy, we are trying to find Mrs Hilda Redford-Hamilton, do you know where she is?" the policewoman asked very casually and cheerfully.

"No," was the stern reply from Carla as she cleaned the pony's body brush with the curry comb. The pony snorted, its hot breath from its fluttering nostrils condensed on the cold air, forming a misty cloud.

"I had a baby last year, when is yours due?" the policewoman gently asked. She could see Carla's bump protruding from her green padded anorak.

Carla turned around and quietly asked, "Does it hurt? I mean childbirth. My friends have told me of horrendous stories about their births and the pain their mothers went through."

"There's all sorts of pain management these days, you will be well looked after."

"It's due in three months, I've tried to hide it from my teachers," Carla stated, replying to the earlier question. She continued to groom her pony.

"Is the dad excited?" Amy asked.

"I don't know, he left when he found out I was pregnant." She turned and continued, "I loved him, I really did. We used to go around shoeing horses and ponies together, I had a great crush on him."

"Ah yes, I remember my first love, I couldn't think of anything else but him," Amy uttered trying to encourage Carla to open up more.

"I led Steve on, you know, I wanted to see what it was like and all that, I thought he would marry me and we could live happily ever after! I'm still crazy about him, I truly ache for him! I hope he will come back to me soon. Do you think he will?"

"He's probably too scared," Amy replied.

"Why because it was under-age sex? It was consensual, he didn't rape me, you know; I encouraged him, I love him with all my heart," Carla shouted, annoyed at the law.

"I know it's hard when everything is against you and the man you love; I was the same – my parents hated my first love."

"What happened?" Carla asked, more relaxed.

"My parents forbade me to never see him again! I hated them for that."

Carla pondered for a while. "At least my parents are standing by me, with my pregnancy I mean... I don't know what they would do if Steve ever came back." Carla bent over and picked up one of the pony's hooves to scrape it out with a hoof pick. She stood up slowly.

"What's breastfeeding like?" Carla asked calmly, stroking her pony's velvety muzzle with such love and affection.

"Wonderful, I highly recommend it, you will make a fantastic mum; I have to go now, I wish you all the best," Amy reassured her.

Carla smiled and the policewoman left to join her colleague who was walking out of the front door.

He told her, "Carla's parents don't know anything about our missing persons. They are naturally furious at the farrier for making their only daughter pregnant and doing a runner. They said they are standing by their daughter and are looking forward to their first grandchild."

The policewoman replied, "It was definitely not rape, Carla still loves him and hopes he will return soon."

Their door-to-door investigations continued – the farm worker who was also a volunteer fireman was visited, but he didn't let them into his cottage. The police stood on the doorstep asking questions – he didn't know anything, nor his family, so they walked on. They met Alan Grey, the glazier, walking up the road and after the small talk they asked, "Did you see a stranger or a white car parked by the church on the grass verge on 29th August 2018?"

"No, can't say I did," Alan replied. He continued on his way to the fire station. The police officers thanked him and headed towards 6 Fell End, down at the end of a cul-de-sac. A flustered, excitable middle-aged woman answered the door. Before they could speak, she hurriedly told them, "Come back tomorrow, Kia is giving birth and the midwife is with her." The rest of the houses in the cul-de-sac didn't reply to their knocks on their doors, so they ambled down the village to 1 Fell Road Cottages and knocked on the blue door.

"Come in, we have been expecting you. We've heard you are doing door-to-door enquiries."

The police officers entered an old-fashioned sitting room, it was dark, so Clara the old lady switched on the main light. Mr Don Barnes was sat in an armchair reading the newspaper near the light from a small lamp.

The police officers asked them the usual questions.

"Ooo, yes I remember! We did give a lift to a girl, well a woman really in her 30s on that date 29th August 2018. We had gone to town to buy a silver money box for our very first great grandchild, didn't we, Don? That was the day little Jack was born! We delivered the rest of his presents, some clothes and booties, ah so tiny! – to our granddaughter's home and had a peep at the wee baby, such a joy–"

"Please could you tell us more about the woman you gave a lift to," interrupted the police officer.

"Of course, we saw her thumbing a lift, didn't we, Don?" Don grunted and folded his newspaper to listen to his wife.

"She was by the old ford. She wondered if we were going to Deadend village; we told her we lived there. She hopped in, she had a small rucksack with her, as I remember. She said she wanted to visit the old church, she told us she used to live here when she was a child and was a junior bell ringer here, the bell tower was a special place to her. She said she would phone for a taxi later to get back into town."

"What time did you drop her off at the church and what was she wearing?"

"Well let me think, it would be about 2 pm, wouldn't it be, Don?"

"Aye, summut like that." Don began to light his pipe.

Clara continued enthusiastically, "She was wearing light blue jeans, a white t-shirt and sandals. A bonny girl, long blonde hair and pretty blue eyes – she told us she was called Cathy Reed, she lived in Newcastle."

"As you passed the church did you see a middle-aged woman with a white car, she had parked it on the grass verge?" the officer asked.

"No, there was no one there or a car, when we dropped Cathy off."

"When did you last see Hilda Redford Hamilton?"

"At the W.I. meeting, I would think. I didn't like her, she tried to take over everything. Did you know we always have a scarecrow festival every summer? She demanded we changed it to flowerpot people, well really! Everyone except the church and vicarages made their scarecrows and had our usual scarecrow fancy dress evening on the pub night. Mrs H.R.H. was furious with us!"

"Serves her right, the silly old bag," murmured Don, unexpectedly. The police officers couldn't help but smile.

"Thank you for your help, you have given us some very useful information," the policeman remarked, pleased they had made some headway at last.

Clara giggled. "Anytime, officers, we are pleased to help."

The police officers chatted in their car for a while.

"That vicar has missed seeing Christine Holmes, the middle-aged woman who ended up in the lake and Cathy Reed. He must be lying; he knows more than he is letting on."

They spoke to the vicar again but he adamantly kept to his story – he hadn't seen anyone that day – 29th August 2018.

Their last interview that day was with the local gossip, Mrs Ackroyd, the woman who had been sacked for rummaging through Hilda Redford-Hamilton's office.

"Horrible woman, she was, evil," Mrs Ackroyd declared.

"Why do you say that, Mrs Ackroyd?"

"Shooting the poor dog and poisoning the defenceless cat, that's why; she was very secretive, had plenty to hide!"

"Did you hear or see anything suspicious?"

"Plenty, I could write a book on it!" she replied, her lips curled into a sly smile.

"We would like to hear any information you may have that will help our investigations."

"Well, I saw her one night, it was gone midnight. I'd got up to get a drink of water, she was prowling around next door! What the devil is she up to, I thought! I quickly dressed and went outside to follow her; she was heading two doors up from me, to Craig Ruddy's house, you know – the artist. She was taking photos and had another instrument, probably a tape recorder, I guess. She wasn't well up on technology, she could have used those phones that the young ones use to take videos …Anyway, when she left, I walked up to where she was standing to see what the Peeping Tom was photographing. There was Craig Ruddy naked as a newborn on top of Wendy Stubbs giving it all–"

"Erm, did you see anything else that Mrs Redford-Hamilton got up to besides being a Peeping Tom?" the police officer asked.

"Well, I thought the photos would be for blackmail, so every time I was in her office cleaning, I'd look for the photos. I saw her peeping into a few houses in the dead of night, like Callum Peach and Gillian Lacey. I learnt a few different positions with that couple, I can tell you! What a steamy affair that was!"

"Erm, did you find anything in her office?"

"Yes, I did! I found out she had a daughter called Elizabeth someone or other, she never comes to see her, so what happened there then? She'd another lah-di-dah name, so Mrs H.R.H. must have married at least twice."

"Is there anything else you can tell us?"

"Well, the vicar and Bill Dobson, I wonder about them an' all! They are frequently at each other's houses–"

"Do you know where Mrs Redford Hamilton is?" interrupted the police officer.

"No, but I did see two men lifting a carpet into a car from her back door, it looked like the vicar's car! I watched him from a distance from the footpath in the field at the back – he drove from The Old Vicarage to his vicarage."

"What date and time was this?"

"I haven't a clue, last summer sometime around dinnertime. Fancy the old cow giving him a carpet, perhaps she didn't like it."

"Who was the other man with him?"

"I'm not sure but it could have been Steve Mann, you know, the farrier. It was the way he walked back to the house, that walk just seemed familiar somehow, he has a stoop."

They returned to the police headquarters to write their reports and set the investigation in motion into the suspected poisoning of Kitty and the alleged forged will. Cathy Reed, the woman who had hitched a ride to the church, was also investigated, joining forces with the Newcastle police force. Cathy Reed could be a vital witness to the middle-aged woman, Christine Holmes, who had visited the bell tower shortly after and who had ended up in the lake in her car. They began their investigations with the taxi services contacting each one, to see if any of them had taken Cathy back into the town.

They also started proceedings to obtain a search warrant for The New Vicarage and the vicar's car.

"This investigation is turning out to be a mammoth task, we need Steve Mann to be interviewed as quickly as possible."

"We haven't interviewed John Milton, the solicitor, and Kate Brown, his secretary, about their blackmail letters," replied the woman police officer.

"We'll interview them tomorrow."

****

Ann and Edward found the work of clearing up the old vicarage and garden a strenuous task, even with the help of the cleaner and gardener.

"I'm realizing that a place this size is too much for us in our old age; we will have to sell it and return to Canada when we can. It was easier living in our small bungalow," Ann grumbled as she prepared a meal for them, after a hard day's work.

"I liked our life before we came here, we're not cut out for this," her husband moaned.

"I hope they find her body soon so we can settle everything up here and go back home," Ann muttered, sighing. She was feeling homesick and was missing her son and daughter and their grandchildren in Canada.

"Hilda might be still alive!" came the reply.

"I doubt it, she wouldn't have left Winston or all her money and finery behind, it's what she lived for to be better than everyone else!" Ann retorted as she served out the meal.

"Delusions of grandeur were her downfall!" Edward remarked. "I think the police should know about the will in the secret compartment in the desk, don't you? We were in Canada when Hilda disappeared. They won't suspect us surely!" Edward exclaimed trying to convince her.

"They would probably think we hired someone to do it, knowing how suspicious they are," Ann sighed.

"If they check our bank accounts, they'll know we didn't send any money to England, it's just our normal pensions going in and general living costs going out."

Ann murmured, "Alright then, I finally agree with you, we'll pop into town tomorrow and let them know. I'll get the original copy of the will later."

Ann had grown very fond of Lotty the cleaner, she thought she was a very capable and a hard-working woman. Lotty told her she was living with her partner; they couldn't afford to marry. They had a daughter called Annie. Lotty loved The Old Vicarage, she had told Ann that if she owned it, she would turn it into a small care home for the elderly.

"It's a shame seeing the elderly having to move out of Deadend village to the care home in town," she remarked. "People that have been born and bred here should be able to stay and be cared for amongst the people they love and know and the village they are familiar with, shouldn't they?" Lotty asked.

"That's a lovely idea, Lotty, how thoughtful you are. I agree, a huge place like this is wasted on just one person."

The following day, Ann retrieved Hilda's will from the bureau desk and handed it to the police detective.

"I had no idea I was the beneficiary of Hilda's will but I remembered the secret compartment in our grandfather's bureau desk."

"Thank you for handing it in. You realize that as this is a murder inquiry, we must make sure this is authentic and make some inquiries to eliminate you from our investigations."

"Yes, I realize that, I'm very willing to help in any way I can," replied Ann.

****

The leading detective was at the front of the packed incident room at the headquarters. He was tall and slim with a greying moustache and a receding hairline; he wore black framed spectacles.

"We know that Mrs Redford-Hamilton was alive and well at 12 noon when Lotty finished cleaning for her at The Old Vicarage on Wednesday, 29th August 2018 and was never seen again. Cathy Reed was dropped off at the church about 2 pm, and we have calculated Christine Holmes arrived there at around 2.30 pm. The vicar claims he didn't see anyone. Now where did these women go?" He was thinking out loud. "Christine Holmes was found in her car in the lake, we know that much... We have been in touch with Newcastle police headquarters, and they say Cathy Reed left home after a violent incident with her husband. She had told her family she was going away for a while to get her 'head straightened out'; no one has heard from her since. She was eventually listed as a missing person. We have no leads on the whereabouts of Mrs Redford-Hamilton so far." He pointed to Steve Mann's name on the white board. "The police in Cornwall tried to interview Steve Mann but his landlady told them he had moved out several days before. He had sold his Land Rover, trailer and equipment and had bought a car. She told them he was working on construction sites in the area. The local police are continuing their search for him."

A police officer in the middle of the room spoke up. "I've heard that Kitty died through the night, we'll have to arrange for an autopsy, to see if she has traces of poison in her body from last summer."

"Oh dear – yes, I'll see to that and the cherry mousse is already being seen to," the leading detective told them all. "How did you come on with the suspect list and any criminal records they may have?" he asked the officer sat on the first row.

"There were only minor driving offences, nothing major."

A young officer spoke up at the back. "The will from Kitty's house was found to be a forgery, here is the letter from the forensic examiner."

"Mmm, looks like Mrs Redford-Hamilton was trying to obtain Kitty's Estate – what did her bank accounts show?"

"I have them here." An older officer passed them forward to the lead detective and continued. "Mrs Redford-Hamilton did not have a large income and she was spending capital to make ends meet."

"It looks like she was getting desperate for money to carry on her lifestyle at The Old Vicarage. She probably didn't want to sell her own material possessions, although she may have had other accounts we don't know about," remarked the leading detective. "We still have John Milton, the solicitor and his secretary Kate Brown to interview about their blackmail letters – I will personally conduct these interviews myself. I will also call in and see Kitty's daughter and update her about the forged will… The vicar's house and car must be investigated by the forensic team as soon as we receive the warrant. We are now waiting for the toxicology test from Kitty's post-mortem and the cherry mousse. Is there anything else?"

A young officer spoke up. "The local taxi services should be asked not only if they took Cathy Reed home but if they also took Mrs Redford-Hamilton out of the village on the same day, when they both disappeared. She may have done a runner!"

"Yes, of course, we must investigate every angle," the lead detective replied.

That evening, the leading detective arrived in the village with a younger detective. They called in on Irene to offer their condolences and to explain to her about Kitty's last will, which had been found to be a forgery.

"I am relieved that my inheritance has not been taken from me, I knew my mother always wanted me to have everything, there are a lot of family heirlooms to pass on," Irene told them as she began to smile with relief.

The detective told her about the post-mortem and the toxicology tests that were being performed to establish if Kitty had indeed been poisoned.

The detectives arrived at Long Fell Barn to interview John Milton, the solicitor. They were invited into the lounge. It was a large room with antique furniture and ornaments. Kate Brown, the solicitor's secretary, was sat there on the settee.

"You're interested in antiques, I see, a passion I share with you," remarked the lead detective to John Milton as he admired the old corner cupboard.

"Yes, most of it I inherited from my mother."

After their discussion, the lead detective began his interview.

"Should I leave?" Kate politely asked.

"This actually concerns both of you, so if you wouldn't mind, we will question you both together. Where is your wife, Mrs Milton?" he asked the solicitor.

"Oh, she is staying with her mother in Sussex for a while – do you wish to interview her as well?"

"No, I didn't want her to interrupt us on this delicate matter that I wish to discuss with you both."

John and Kate glanced at each other; they had a good idea why the detectives were there.

"We have found copies of letters blackmailing both of you about an affair you are having. Did you pay the blackmailer?"

John spoke first. "Yes we did, we followed the instructions in the letter and deposited the cash behind the gravestone at the requested time and date."

Kate added, "We had our reputations at risk. We wouldn't have been accepted in the village, if this got out!"

John joined in. "We have finished our affair; we were just saying goodbye when you rang the doorbell. I hope you will be as discreet as possible about this matter."

The lead detective continued, "We will try. Do you know who was blackmailing you?"

John replied, "No, but I have my suspicions! I think it could possibly have been Hilda Redford-Hamilton, but this is speaking 'off the record' of course."

"Why her?" asked the lead detective.

"She never liked me or Kate, we were perhaps the only ones in the village who stood up to her bullying tactics."

"When did you last see Mrs Redford-Hamilton?"

"It was a long while ago, probably at a church service, our paths didn't cross very often, thank goodness," John replied with a sigh.

"I have no idea when I last saw her, I'm sorry but I can't remember," Kate told them.

"Did you see any strangers in the village or a white car parked on the verge near the church between about 2 to 3 pm on Wednesday 29th August 2018?"

"No," replied John.

Kate added, "No, I saw no one, I would have been at work at that time anyway."

The detective thanked them and left.

Kate looked searchingly into John's worried eyes. "You know something, don't you? You weren't at work that day, were you?"

John abruptly replied, "Don't ask, it's better you know nothing and then you are not involved."

THE RED RUG IS FOUND

The detectives approached The New Vicarage. The vicar had seen their car headlights, he saw their car being parked on the driveway, so he opened the front door. The bright light from the hallway lit up the flagged pathway. The leading detective introduced both of them.

"We have a search warrant to search your premises," the lead detective told the astonished vicar. A van, at that moment, pulled into the driveway; crime scene investigators jumped out and headed to the front door. They were all led into the sitting room where a small log fire was burning in the grate.

"A witness has come forward stating you were seen, with another person, carrying out a red rug from the back door of The Old Vicarage."

"Yes, I did take the rug. I had permission from Mrs Redford-Hamilton," he explained. He was alarmed at possibly being accused of theft. "She had bought it for her dining room but didn't like the way the red fibres were shedding onto her white carpet."

"Can you show me the rug?"

"Of course, it's through here in the meeting room." The rug was laid in front of the large table and chairs. Photos were taken of it in situ.

"We will have to take it away for analysis. When did you remove the rug from the other vicarage?"

"I'm not sure, it was before Mrs Redford-Hamilton left."

"You were seen carrying the rug with another man. Surely it's not that heavy – one man could have taken it to the boot of your car."

The vicar didn't reply.

"Who was the other man helping you?"

"Steve Mann, the farrier, he's no longer living in the village," he nervously answered.

"Do you know where he lives?"

"No, sorry I don't," came the reply.

The crime scene investigators bagged up the rug and began the search of the house.

"Did Mrs Redford-Hamilton ever come inside this house?" the leading detective asked.

"Very rarely... Am I a suspect?"

"Everyone is a suspect until they are eliminated from our inquiries," replied the detective.

The team began to investigate the room for blood, tissue and hair. A hair was found snagged in a partial splinter in the wood frame at the side of the backrest of the armchair. It was carefully removed, the tiny hair follicle on the end could just be seen. The vicar felt very nervous, that was the chair Christine Holmes had sat in while she drank her sugared tea and a biscuit covered in – what Christine thought was icing sugar.

Once they had finished in the meeting room, they crossed the hall into the sitting room. The vicar looked agitated and was shocked he was being investigated like this. He sat in his brown leather armchair watching what they were doing. They appeared to be looking for blood and tissue on the well-trodden terracotta-coloured carpet. They even moved his armchair to look at the carpet underneath. The team also examined the fire tools hung on the stand by the open fire.

The vicar watched as each tool was examined carefully. The tongs appeared to suggest there was blood present; the tiny area was swabbed, chemicals were added to the swab, he could see it turn rapidly into a bright pink, in colour. The vicar was informed there was blood present.

"It's most probably mine, I'm always cutting myself," he told them as calmly as he could. The tongs were photographed, bagged and tagged for further analysis.

They all walked back into the hallway where another crime scene investigator had been examining the carpet and walls for traces of blood, tissue and hair.

They walked into the vicar's office.

"I see you have two computers – are they both yours?" the leading detective asked in a sombre tone.

"Yes, this one is for church work and this is my own personal computer," the vicar replied uneasily.

"We will have to take them, to check them out, but you will have them back soon if we no longer need them for evidence." The vicar was shocked but didn't protest. Photos were taken of the two computers sitting on the old desk.

All the vicar's papers in his desk were examined and a box file with the number seven was retrieved from the cupboard on the right-hand side of the desk.

"Is this yours?" asked the detective.

"Err, yes it belongs with my other box files on this shelf here."

There were eight box files and a gap where this seventh box file was missing. The file was opened, but it contained only notes for church business. The detective had first thought it was the missing file from Mrs Redford-Hamilton's office. The other box files were searched, the carpet and walls were examined, but no evidence was found.

They walked into the kitchen area, where there was a wooden table and four chairs in the middle of the room. A six-piece knife set was stood on the unit top which immediately caught their eye. Each knife was taken out and examined closely. The room was examined thoroughly, even towels and tea towels were scrutinized for blood stains.

Upstairs, each bedroom was systematically searched. In the bottom of a wardrobe in the vicar's own room they found a camera.

"Does this camera belong to you?" the vicar was asked. The detective wondered if it was the missing camera from Hilda's house.

"Yes, the receipt should still be in the case as I bought it only a few weeks ago."

The detective checked and indeed there was a crumpled-up receipt at the bottom of the brown case. He read the date – it did prove he was telling the truth.

The plain white bathroom was examined, but nothing suspicious was found in there.

"Do you have an attic?"

"Yes, come this way." The vicar pulled the hatch door open with a hooked rod and pulled down the wooden step ladder.

The team and the leading detective ascended the ladders.

"The light switch is on the left at floor level," the vicar advised them. A thorough search was made through all the boxes using their torches. A big oak chest stood out amongst all the items.

"This chest is locked, have you got the key?" shouted the lead detective to the vicar below.

"I'll fetch it for you." He went into his bedroom followed by the other detective, to retrieve it.

The chest was opened, the leading detective pulled out one of the long black cloaks and a black full-faced leather mask. He looked puzzled.

"What are these?" he shouted down to the vicar.

"Oh, there's about half a dozen of them, they're costumes for a church play," he shouted back up into the attic as casually as he could.

After the search they all congregated in the sitting room. The crime scene investigators left to search the car after they had obtained the keys from the vicar. In the boot, there were lots of red fibres found; they would be able to see if they matched the fibres on the vicar's carpet rug. There was no blood, dark brown hair or human tissue found in the car.

"Are you willing to give a DNA sample and fingerprints to eliminate you from our enquiries?" asked the lead detective.

"Of course, anything I can do to help," replied the vicar. Once it was completed, the detectives and crime scene investigators left with the items they had bagged and tagged. The police didn't have enough evidence yet to arrest him on anything but they knew he was lying about a few things.

****

"I'm fed up of this telephone ringing, I must have had 20 telephone calls from the press wanting me to give an interview!" Ann exclaimed, standing in the lounge at The Old Vicarage.

"Just leave it ringing," her placid husband replied.

She ignored him and went over to the phone, picked the receiver up and immediately plonked it down.

"At last, a bit of peace! They were even at the door today, I gave them 'sharp shrift' I can tell you, well really, as if we had any idea of where Hilda is or why she's missing."

"Fred told me, while we were mending the garden shed – a spade was missing! Did you know all Hilda's tools are engraved with her initials H.R.H.?"

"It's a wonder she doesn't have a coat of arms hung over the front door," Ann replied in a sarcastic voice.

"I think I should tell the police, don't you? It may be the spade that was used to bury her!" Edward sounded very worried.

"Well it could be, or someone just borrowed it, it could have even been stolen, I suppose," Ann replied, pushing up her bi-vocals on her nose.

"I'll let the police know when I see them," he replied. At least it would relieve him of the worry, he thought to himself.

****

It was a lively pub night in the village hall, people had plenty of gossip to talk about.

"Poor Kitty, my mum and her went to the village school together. It's a while since the post-mortem, has anyone heard any results?" shouted May, who lived almost opposite Kitty at Fell Face Terrace.

"They found traces of poisons in her tissues and the same poisons in that cherry mousse – Irene told me when I saw her yesterday. Mrs H.R.H. must have concocted a cocktail of poisons. Irene also told me it's Kitty's funeral tomorrow, everyone is invited, she says she's invited the detectives as well, there'll be plenty of food in the village hall after," Lily informed everyone.

"Can they pin this poisoning and fraud on Mrs H.R.H. then?" asked another woman stood holding her glass of gin and tonic.

"Well, it was Mrs Redford-Hamilton's name written on the forged will, she was supposed to be the sole beneficiary to Kitty's money and property and it was her that gave the poisoned cherry mousse to Kitty. So, when they find her, she'll be up for attempted murder and fraud!" declared an angry feisty woman wiping down a table.

"Serves her right, she had plenty to sell – why did she need to take from others?" Joe Thur announced, extremely annoyed.

"Likely to keep up appearances and status, it was all about being better than us, wasn't it?" added Mildred, holding her port and lemon.

"Aye," was the reply from a unison of voices in the room.

"What were they doing at The New Vicarage?" Fred asked, when there was a pause in the conversation.

"It looked as if they had the forensic team or something there. I suppose he does live next door; do you think they will be searching everyone's house?" Jim asked.

A young man holding a pint of beer replied, "The police have to have some suspicious evidence to be able to get a warrant for a search."

"I told them about the red rug carpet I saw the vicar taking out of the back door of The Old Vicarage with another man, possibly Steve Mann. Now why would they take it out of that door when the dining room is nearer the front door, unless they were hiding something!" Mrs Ackroyd announced.

"They'll be suspecting they were carrying out Mrs H.R.H.'s body!" laughed another. Then the whole room erupted with laughter from everyone.

"Edward Harrison told the police one of her spades out of the garden shed is missing, it's got her initials engraved on it, so they'll know it's hers, if they find it," Fred, the gardener, added.

"Aye, she's buried somewhere, the spade will have been left with her, I suppose. I wonder who could've done it?" Jim asked.

"The police would think anyone of us could've killed her, we all hated her for different reasons!"

"Yer right there, do you remember we were holding a meeting in her posh dining room and time was running short. We were about to do a democratic vote on who was to be the next treasurer when she just pointed to Sally and said, 'you'll do, you're good at maths'."

Sally joined in. "Yes, and I didn't even want the job!"

"I hated the way she used to bang on the table with her hand, 'listen, listen to me' she used to say in her foghorn voice," a woman said, mimicking Hilda's voice. There was another bout of laughter from everyone in the village hall.

"Mrs H.R.H. always wanted to be the centre of attention."

"Remember all those sherry mornings, coffee mornings, garden parties – her strutting about looking like a proud peacock, like she was royalty or something," Gail remarked.

Mildred spoke up. "Well, she did raise a lot of money for charity with those events. Give her credit where credit is due."

Lily laughed and replied, "Unless she pocketed it all for herself!"

Everyone laughed till their sides ached. "She started off all right when she first came – she donated the rest of the money we couldn't raise for this place; it badly needed a new roof. It must have been tens of thousands of pounds," John stated, taking a sip of lager.

"She did that to get well into the community and then she started taking over as if she was like that woman in 'To the manor born' or something."

"Yer right there, too big for her own boots at times."

People began to leave the hall; it was late. The wind was howling around the outside of the building, it was also sleeting heavily. It would be a miserable walk home for everyone.

****

During the night there was a heavy snowfall, and the village was totally cut off from the main road.

"See if you can get the council to go in with a snowplough or something, tell them we are conducting a police investigation there and need access to the village," the leading detective asked a police officer. He continued, "In the meantime we'll have a meeting in the incident room."

Everyone who was available entered the room.

"We'll have a recap. As you all know it is Kitty's funeral today; myself and Jim will attend on behalf of the police force. The road to the village is blocked with snow at present, but hopefully the council will deal with it shortly. Now back to business – the trace of blood on the vicar's tongs has been found to be his own blood as it was a match to his DNA sample that was taken. His computers were returned as they definitely were not the computer stolen from Mrs Redford-Hamilton's house. However, the DNA from the hair follicle found on the armchair at The New Vicarage, matched Christine Holmes' DNA. Detectives had saved samples of her hair taken from her brush, when she was reported missing by her sister. Fortunately, there was also hair follicles present to compare the DNA."

Another detective spoke out. "It could have been transferred from the church tower onto the vicar's clothes and then to the armchair."

"Yes, it is possible, but it will allow us to bring the vicar to the police headquarters for questioning. We'll be able to record everything." He looked down at his list. "Did anyone ask if there was a play using black robes and masks?"

"Yes, I did, I asked the main organizer of the entertainment's committee, a Mrs Milly Oldham. She said there had been no plays or pantomimes in the past or presently being arranged that require those sorts of costumes."

"So, the vicar is lying again! It was unlikely they would use expensive full-faced leather masks for costumes – it's usually felt, isn't it?"

"Yes, or black painted cardboard," another officer suggested.

"We now come to the red rug carpet and the red fibres in the boot of the vicar's car. They were a match. I had wondered if they were in fact two different rug carpets involved here but this proves otherwise. There was no DNA found from Mrs Redford-Hamilton in the car or on the rug carpet and fibres. We are back to square one where she is concerned," sighed the lead detective as he scanned his list again.

A police officer added, "Edward Harrison informed me that a spade with a wooden shaft, had been stolen from the garden shed at The Old Vicarage, it has H.R.H. engraved on the shaft. It could have been used as a murder weapon or to bury her, or both."

"So, we have a spade, a computer, a camera, a tape recorder and a box file marked with a number 7 and a front door key missing from Mrs Redford-Hamilton's house. In her pocket she usually had a mobile phone – most probably turned off. There have been no sightings of her since 29th August 2018 and she hasn't used any of her bank accounts that we know about. She didn't take a taxi out of the village, we know that... There is plenty of motive for murder – she blackmailed eight people, attempted murder of Kitty and forged her will. She definitely wasn't liked in the village for taking control of everything."

"What about Cathy Reed? Do we know any more regarding her?" asked a police officer stood at the back of the room.

"We know she had a lift on that day to the church at about 2 pm. Christine Holmes hadn't arrived by then, she arrived about 2.30 pm. They were both going to the bell tower so it's very likely they would have met each other. Christine Holmes left but no one saw her leave in her car which ended up in the lake. There is no record of Cathy Reed taking a taxi back into town."

"What if Christine Holmes gave a lift to Cathy Reed and there was some kind of disagreement, Cathy got out and Christine later skidded into the lake?"

"If Cathy Reed was walking alone on the main road she would have been seen, her photo is everywhere. Also, she had her mobile phone with her to ring for a taxi. No, my instincts tell me something went on in that bell tower..."

and now we have found these black cloaks and masks, I think it's something to do with the occult; I know the vicar is involved with it all somehow... How have the police in Cornwall come on looking for Steve Mann?"

"They haven't found him yet, he is using various aliases," a police officer replied.

"What about Mrs Redford-Hamilton's daughter? Have we any leads on her?" the lead detective asked.

"I'm struggling with her, I traced her to Coventry but I'll have to make some more phone calls," called out another officer.

"We need something, the door-to-door enquiries have now been completed and no more leads have come up – this investigation is stalling. I will bring back in the vicar for a recorded interview after the funeral, see if we can pressure him into revealing any more information."

****

The roads had been cleared by the snow plough; heaps of snow formed a white glistening wall either side of the single-track road. Villagers had done their best to shovel pathways through to their homes and to the church. The school bus had been cancelled as the snow hadn't been removed for the school bus in time, the village school was also closed. The local farmer had cleared the car park around the village hall using his tractor with a fore end loader and bucket. The detectives parked there and walked down the slippery road to the church. The black hearse eventually arrived carrying Kitty in her coffin from the chapel of rest in the town, where her body had been placed after her post-mortem.

At the entrance to the church, the tall, black double wrought iron gates had been lifted off their metal hooks and propped up against the wall and railings. They had been secured by a rope to prevent them falling over. The gateway wasn't wide enough with the gates hung to accommodate the village pall bearers carrying the coffin. The path had been cleared and was well gritted for their slow walk to the church.

A large spray of white lilies lay on top of the dark wooden coffin. The mood was sombre as the cortege followed behind the coffin. In the church the coffin was placed carefully on a wooden stand. It was a very moving service about a woman who had played a great part in the village community.

The lead detective wondered what she would have thought of the investigation ongoing in the village, if she could have comprehended what was going on in her final days. She was very lucky she didn't die from the poisoning – it was her dislike for cherries that had saved her life, the previous August. He looked around while joining in the hymns, he recognized a few faces. Anyone of them could have killed Mrs Redford-Hamilton, he thought to himself, they were no nearer to solving the case.

Kitty's great granddaughter, a teenager, read a poem she had written. It was very heartfelt and moving, a few people quietly cried. He could see this community was very close and Kitty had been well loved.

Outside it was bitterly cold stood in the cemetery. The family huddled together near the coffin listening to the vicar saying a prayer. Slowly the coffin was lowered to its final resting place, and flowers were thrown onto the coffin. The gravediggers must have had to have had the grave dug in the finer weather, he thought to himself, as his feet began to go cold in his thin-soled shoes.

The cortege moved away from the graveside, to the church path, to the waiting cars. They were taken to the wake, held in the village hall. The detectives walked back up the road, looking forward to the warmth of the indoors.

Irene thanked them for coming. "Come and see the food. The villagers have created a wonderful spread, there are apple pies baked by Mildred — she always bakes the old-fashioned way with cloves, they are delicious. These are the sausage rolls I made, there are lots of sandwiches, cakes and desserts friends have brought. Please help yourselves."

It was all laid out on trestle tables covered in white sheets, around the sides of the room. The detectives mingled with the mourners holding their plates full of food, the atmosphere was more relaxed and cheerful. As they meandered through the packed hall of people, they heard snippets of conversation.

"Aye, Tommy managed to get grave dug before bad weather, he'll be filling it in nar wi Mick's Bobcat digger," John remarked, as he chatted to Alan Grey.

"She had a good life, bless her..."

"Yes, Kia's doing fine, her baby is feeding well..."

There was a table dedicated to the memory of Kitty's life, her black and white baby photos and photos of her life as she grew into a young woman, the war years when she was a land girl, her wedding and the child she had. Silver cups for winning at bowls were displayed together with a quilt which was hung on the wall. She had obviously spent many hours painstakingly making it.

The detectives had noticed the vicar leave, so after they had finished eating, they excused themselves and left the hall. The wind was bitingly cold on their cheeks as they strode out towards their car. They got in and drove to The New Vicarage and knocked on the door. The vicar opened it, he looked drained as if he hadn't slept the previous night.

"We would like you to accompany us to the police station, we have more questions to ask you."

The vicar looked confused. "I thought I'd told you everything you wished to know!"

"It won't take long, just a few ends to clear up."

"I'll get my coat," the vicar replied. He was silent most of the way, he was nervous about what questions they had lined up for him and he knew he would be recorded.

****

Later in the afternoon the craft and chat group had assembled in Gill's house.

"I thought we would have our club meeting in here, they'll still be tidying up the hall after Kitty's wake."

"It's cosy in here, I've brought some knitting, now I know Kia's had a baby girl, I thought I would knit some pink bonnets, mitts and bootees."

"What a good idea, I gave her a handmade pink and white toy rabbit, I got it from Julie's white box. I swapped it for a fruit cake, I know Julie loves my special fruit cakes," Jane remarked, picking up her embroidery.

Sally got out her needlework from her bag. "Hey, do you think they will ever find Mrs H.R.H.? It's all in the papers and on the telly but their investigation doesn't appear to be going anywhere."

"Those detectives were seen heading towards The New Vicarage, I wonder if they arrested the vicar!" Carol remarked.

"At least they waited till after the funeral!" Gill exclaimed.

"Milly told me they were asking her about black cloaks and masks, if they were for a play. Where would they find those?" Carol asked.

"Well, they've only searched the church and the two vicarages so far, so they must have found them in one of those places," came the reply from Jane.

"Do you think there's a witches' coven in the village?" Gill asked, lowering her voice to create a mystical atmosphere.

"No, everyone would know about it, don't they dance around naked in graveyards and woods or something?" asked Mary laughing, joining in the gossip.

Sally looked up in surprise. "I don't think any of the villagers would be into that, we're all quite religious really."

THE INTERVIEW AND THE BODY

"Take a seat," the lead detective suggested kindly, pointing to a chair.

The vicar sat down and looked around the small, windowless interview room; he'd never been interviewed at a police station before. After the introductions were made for the recording, the questions began.

"Now on the date of 29th August 2018, you have stated on numerous occasions, you didn't see anyone that day. Do you recall anything now?" the senior detective asked in a mild tone of voice.

"No," was the vicar's short response.

"Tells us from the beginning what you did after leaving The New Vicarage after your breakfast on that day," continued the detective.

The vicar replied after a moment of thought, "I stayed indoors for a while after breakfast to make a few phone calls, as I remember."

A question flew back at him immediately, the tone was starting to become more serious. "Who were the phone calls to?"

"I can't really remember, possibly to my bank and maybe to the organist. I then went outside as it was a lovely day. There had been a wedding the previous Saturday, and although I'd swept up the confetti, there were still traces of it left, it gets everywhere, so I tidied the rest of it up."

"Then what did you do?" the senior detective abruptly asked.

"I walked around the grounds and the graveyard to see that everything was in order and went back indoors for a cup of coffee. I read the newspaper and returned to the church. I had decided to repair a shelf in one of the storerooms. Then it was lunchtime so I returned to the vicarage," the vicar replied feeling uncomfortable being questioned.

"What time was this?" the senior detective demanded in an annoyed way.

"About twelve," the vicar replied, crossing his legs. A behaviour suggesting to the detectives he was lying and feeling vulnerable.

"What did you do after lunch?" the other detective quickly asked.

The vicar folded his arms, he had barely time to think. "I returned to the church."

"What time was this?"

"About one," the vicar continued. "I wanted to do some weeding around the church walls as I'd noticed when I'd swept up the confetti, the weeds were getting out of control – the volunteer groundsman was absent due to a long illness," he told them, hoping he wouldn't get confused about his alibi.

"Whereabouts were you weeding between 2 and 3 pm?"

"Possibly at the far end away from the main door at the other side of the church," the vicar replied in a quiet voice. He was lying.

"Could you have heard or seen anyone park a car on the grass verge and walk up the church path, open the main door and shut it behind them?"

"I wouldn't think so where I was working," came the meek reply.

"Did you hear or see anyone else?"

"No." He had to continue lying, which was becoming very stressful for him.

"Did you hear two women talking in the church or outside?"

"No, I was concentrating on my weeding, I heard no one."

"How long did the weeding take you?"

"I'm not sure, I wanted to relieve myself so I went back home and while I was there, I had a cup of tea and read the rest of the newspaper." He was beginning to sweat under the pressure and wished they didn't go into so much detail.

"Then what did you do?"

"I had been working at the far end of the church, so I walked back to continue weeding until teatime at five. About six that evening, I was making notes for a sermon, which I wrote up, then I sat and watched the TV." He lowered his eyes to the floor and looked up as the next question was quickly 'fired' at him.

"What did you watch on the TV?"

"I haven't a clue, it was a long time ago, I can't remember," he protested. He was shocked at the abrupt way he was being questioned, he was there voluntarily, he was not under arrest.

"Did the telephone ring at all that evening?"

"Not that I can recall, no," he replied. He knew full well he hadn't been at the vicarage that evening. The police knew Christine Holme's sister was urgently trying to contact him and he should've heard the telephone ringing.

"Did you go out at all?"

"No, not that I remember." Another blatant lie he had to tell, he was getting deeper and deeper into a mire with his story of lies.

"When did you remove the red rug from Mrs Redford-Hamilton's house?"

"I can't remember the exact date, but it was before she left."

"Why did you take it out of the back door when the dining room where it lay, is nearer to the front door?" the detective demanded to know.

"Mrs Redford-Hamilton had already moved it out of her dining room – she didn't like the red fibres shedding from the rug, it was messing up her white carpet. She had rolled it up and had left it lying on the stone slab in the boot room at the back of the house. She had asked me on the phone a few days earlier, if I wanted it for the vicarage, and I said, 'yes'. I told her I would collect it." He hoped that would satisfy them.

"Why did it take two of you to lift the carpet rug into your car?"

"Steve Mann was already at the house; he came into the boot room when I arrived and he just grabbed hold of the end of the carpet and I did the same at the other end. He was just being helpful, I suppose. We took it to the boot of my car."

"Why was Steve Mann at the house?"

"He said he was moving the white appliances around in the utility room for Mrs Redford-Hamilton."

"Was Mrs Redford-Hamilton there with you as you moved the carpet?"

"Yes, she was stood in the boot room watching us."

"What did you and Steve Mann do next?"

"Steve went back into the boot room and I left."

"Why did Steve Mann return to the boot room?"

"I don't know, probably to be paid in cash."

"We asked the main organizer of the entertainment's committee, Mrs Milly Oldham, about the cloaks and masks. She told us that they'd not been used in any plays or pantomimes or would be in the future, yet you told us otherwise."

"I can explain that. When I moved in about five years ago, I found the chest in the attic; it was locked. I was intrigued about what could be inside it, I hadn't been given a key. I searched the attic and found the key tucked into a crevice in the stone wall. When I saw what was inside, I just assumed they were costumes for a play."

"Do you know of any occult practices going on in the village?"

"No, the villagers are all 'God fearing people', as far as I know."

"Christine Holmes, the middle-aged woman who came to visit the bell tower on 29th August 2018, who you claimed you never saw, and who ended up in the lake; had her DNA in your vicarage – your home. The hair follicle was found on the armchair in the meeting room and it matched her DNA taken from the hair follicles in her brush she had at her sister's house, where she was staying."

The vicar shook his head from side to side.

"I didn't see her that day! I don't know how her hair got into my home! I can only say it could have landed on me when I was in the church or the bell tower and it came off later in my house." He tried desperately to sound convincing.

"How often do you go into the bell tower?"

"Rarely, but I was there that day the police came to investigate the church. I also sometimes 'fill in' if someone is unable to attend bell ringing – I was a bell ringer in my youth."

"Did you do any bell ringing between 29th August 2018 up until when the hair follicle was found in your meeting room?"

"Yes, the dates will be in my diary."

"Did you originally come from Deadend village?"

"Yes, I was born and bred there and so was my father and grandfather and generations before them. I left for a while for my training at a theological college. My calling has always been to become ordained in the church like my grandfather – he used to live at The Old Vicarage when he was the vicar of this parish."

"Do you know of any secret passages or rooms in The Old Vicarage?"

"Yes, I do. I believe a secret room in the inner hall is used as a broom cupboard."

"Do you know of any more secret rooms or passages?"

"No."

"When did your homosexual affair begin with the organist?"

"What's that got to do with the disappearance of Mrs Redford-Hamilton?"

"Answer the question please," came an abrupt reply.

"Two years, we have kept it very discreet as we didn't think the villagers would understand; they are very set in their ways, particularly the older generation. I hope this will go no further."

"As long as the affair has nothing to do with the disappearance of these women and is not involved in anything we are investigating, then I see no reason why your relationship should be made public. Do you know if the person was blackmailing anyone else in the village and do you know who the blackmailer is?"

"No, I don't," the vicar snapped.

"Have you had anything to do with the disappearance of Mrs Redford-Hamilton or Cathy Reed, or anything to do with Christine Holmes and her ending up in the lake?"

"No, absolutely not," the vicar replied in alarm; he knew full well he had.

"Do you know anyone who has?"

"No, definitely not."

"Is there anything else you wish to tell us?"

"I can't think of anything right now but if I do, I'll let you know."

The detectives thanked him for his time and arranged for him to be driven home.

The detectives thought his story sounded plausible on the surface but knew from his body language and sweating, he was telling lies.

They would have to check out his story, about 'filling in' as a bell ringer between the two dates mentioned, because the day the police searched the bell tower, the vicar was nowhere near the armchair in the meeting room – the interview was conducted in the kitchen: so, it was unlikely for a transfer of the hair follicle to happen on that occasion. When the search at The New Vicarage took place, they knew he had sat in his own leather armchair in his sitting room but not the other armchair in the meeting room.

The vicar was very relieved to arrive home. He didn't like lying, he felt very nervous, he knew the detectives didn't believe him. They obviously had no hard evidence or he would have been arrested by now, he pondered to himself. He phoned Bill Dobson, the organist, who was also his lover – he had to talk to someone in confidence, he felt very distressed.

Police officers quickly found out that the vicar had 'filled in' for Jenny, when she was on holiday for two weeks; this was within the specific dates. So, there was a possibility of the hair follicle being transferred to the armchair but to the detectives, this was highly unlikely. They were frustrated that no bodies had been found apart from Christine Holmes' in her car found in the lake. They knew she had been in Deadend village as her DNA was on the armchair. The case had no hard evidence to convict anyone at this stage – it was stalling fast!

****

Village life continued, the snow had started to thaw and the crocuses were starting to bud in the gardens and in the grass verges.

"Are you going to the buffet club today, Julie?" asked Milly who was walking up the road with her little Jack Russell terrier.

"Yes, I've made a quiche to take, how about you – what are you taking?" Julie replied.

"I've made some little meat and potato pasties. It's a good idea this buffet club gets us all out for a good chat and a lovely meal too."

"Yes, and we raise more than enough to pay the running costs on the hall, with our £1 entrance fee. I'm going to the activity club now, why don't you join us, the instructors are very good."

"I'm too old!" Milly exclaimed, wrinkling up her nose.

"Mildred goes and she's older than you!"

At the activity club the ages ranged from 40 to 90 years old! There was a warm up and simple exercises that everyone could do at their own pace. After a cup of tea and cakes it was time for games, Curling (on wheels), table tennis, badminton and sit-down bowls. They had time to relax and chat before the buffet club.

"Is that old couple from Canada staying at The Old Vicarage permanently?" asked Sue.

"Lotty says, 'not', they are only staying until things are sorted," replied Brenda.

"I had a go at Mrs Ackroyd yesterday, she was telling lies again about Wendy Stubbs and Craig Ruddy having an affair! I told her not to tell lies, and she replied, 'I don't tell lies, I may exaggerate to emphasize my point but I never lie' – she then stormed off in a huff."

Brenda laughed. "You never know when she is telling the truth, she is such a gossip."

The buffet club was a thriving enterprise, the hall was generally full of village folk, tables and chairs were set out for the meal for those who needed to sit down. It was every Wednesday lunchtime for anyone, as long as they brought something and paid their £1 at the door.

"Who do you think murdered Mrs H.R.H. then?" Margaret asked Carol while she ate a sausage roll.

Carol pondered for a while. "It could've been the solicitor, John Milton. He was always arguing with her, he and his secretary, what's 'er name – Kate Brown – could've done it, they were probably the only ones who could stand up to her."

Betty replied, "He thinks he is so important but he's only a conveyancing solicitor, he doesn't work in the courts."

"I think she's just gone AWOL," announced Jenny. "She's probably found a rich aristocrat and scarpered!" They all laughed.

Margaret suggested, "Perhaps she's gone somewhere, had an accident and totally lost her memory."

"She would've taken her vehicle to get out of the village – it's still standing on her driveway," Carol replied, tucking into a lemon mousse.

"The police haven't a clue or they would've arrested someone by now if she's been murdered," uttered Jenny, spilling her coffee down her blue jumper. "Oops, I don't know where my mouth is these days!"

"I think it's Steve Mann, he scarpered, didn't he? It was soon after Mrs H.R.H. disappeared, I bet the police are after him," Jane suggested, picking up her slice of lemon drizzle cake from her plate.

"He's done a runner because he got Carla Robinson in the family way and it was under-aged sex!" exclaimed Mary.

Fiona spoke up. "I think it's the vicar, he is the only one to have his house searched and he's been questioned at the police station."

"Why would the vicar murder Mrs H.R.H.?" asked Betty, sounding very alarmed.

"Maybe she had something on him and he murdered her to shut her up!"

"A man of the cloth wouldn't do such a thing," May retorted, very shocked.

Fiona lowered her voice and asked, "Do you think Mrs H.R.H. had anything to do with old Bob's death? She was taking food around to him last August after Gail's cat was poisoned. He had similar symptoms to poor old Kitty last August before Mrs H.R.H. disappeared. She also took some cherry mousse around to him just as she did with Kitty!"

"He hadn't any money or property and his son from town would be the beneficiary to his will, I think. So why would she kill him, she wasn't going to gain by it?" Betty replied, unsettled at the allegations.

"I think you should mention it to the police, Fiona, you never know what she could've been up to," Mary urged.

Kia walked in just then with her baby girl, and everyone turned to greet her.

"Aw, she's so cute," Jenny cooed as she looked into the baby's buggy.

"There's plenty of people to babysit if ever you want a night out, love, we are after all one big happy family here," Brenda happily suggested to her.

"Aye, I bet we're all related along the line somehow," laughed Jenny.

"It's lovely to have some good news in the village to cheer us up, it's been so depressing what with the weather, all the police investigations and Kitty's funeral," Margaret remarked, holding the baby's tiny hand covered in her little pink mitten.

After lunch was cleared, it was the film club. Today they would be paying to watch 'Sense and Sensibility' by Jane Austen, with a break in the middle for a cup of tea and cakes. Many stayed on for the domino night.

"I love Wednesdays, there is so much going on," Julie remarked.

"I agree, we have a very vibrant village here, there is something on every day to go to and see friends. There's something for everyone to do," replied Carol.

Fiona plucked up the courage to ring the police about old Bob. "I don't know whether the information I have is of any significance to your investigations at Deadend village, but I thought I would ring and let you know." Fiona told her story about Mrs Redford-Hamilton taking food to Bob Waldon at his house, like she had done with Kitty. Bob died a few days later from similar symptoms.

"He has a son, Tim Waldon, the printer in the town, next to the jeweller's shop. You could ask him for details," Fiona informed the police officer.

"Thank you for your information, we will definitely follow it up," the police officer replied, grateful for another lead.

****

Twenty miles away two experienced and well 'kitted out' walkers were trekking through the lonely countryside; one of them spotted what looked like part of a blonde wig near some bushes.

The hair was matted in the mud and partly covered with leaves. They walked closer and peered down at the strange phenomenon, then realized to their horror –

"It's a body!" cried the male walker in total shock.

The couple quickly stepped back in fear, startled by the sight of the grizzly scene. The corpse was badly decomposed apart from the lower half; they could see a pair of light blue jeans, still intact. A pair of sandals lay nearby, partly under a gorse bush.

"We should phone the police immediately," the female walker suggested, her face full of terror at what she was witnessing.

The male walker quickly fumbled nervously in his pocket for his mobile phone and rung the police. In a distraught voice he explained about the decomposing body and told them roughly where it was situated.

The couple stayed in the area to help direct the police to the body. They thought they would light a small campfire about 100 yards from the remains behind a dry stone wall near to the road; it would shelter them and help them to keep warm from the bitterly cold gusts of wind; the smoke would also alert the police to the exact place. They took water from the nearby stream and boiled it in a can over the campfire, the hot liquid would help keep their body cores warm. The police took about an hour to arrive on the scene; they started to process the area. The detectives questioned the walkers at length before they were allowed to go.

After the area was searched around the body for scattered bones, the body parts and scattered bones were photographed and placed in a body bag and evidence bags. The body bag was laid on a stretcher and taken to a waiting police vehicle.

There was no skull, only a few rib bones, vertebrae and a few bones from the arms and hands. The lower part of the body was partially intact dressed in jeans, and a clump of blonde hair lay where her head would have been. Wild animals and perhaps crows had torn and picked at the body and scattered the bones from the upper torso.

The police in the town involved in the investigation in Deadend village, began to suspect it was Cathy Reed; they needed this break to further their investigations. The remains had blonde hair and was wearing light blue jeans and a pair of sandals, similar to what Cathy Reed was last seen wearing. They forewarned her distressed family about the possible link to the decomposed body before it was splashed on the front pages of the newspapers.

The detectives waited patiently for the DNA results to be compared to the DNA sample of hair in Cathy Reed's brush and comb, which was taken when she had been reported as a missing person from Newcastle. It wasn't a match. Her anxious family were greatly relieved on hearing the news – they were still clinging onto the hope she would return home unharmed.

The decomposing corpse was later identified as a 20-year-old, who was last seen at a party at 3 am, months ago – she didn't have anything to do with Deadend village or their investigations.

The police were totally frustrated that they had no more leads, but they did know that Mrs Redford-Hamilton and Cathy Reed had not left the village in a taxi. They knew something had happened in the bell tower that day, 29th August 2018, but they didn't know what.

****

Tim Waldon was questioned by the police. His father, Bob Waldon, had been buried in the village cemetery. He had died intestate as he had no assets of value, so he didn't think it was worth making a will. It was the symptoms before death that had alerted the police and the fact Mrs Redford-Hamilton was delivering food to his house including cherry mousse. They decided to have the corpse exhumed for forensic analysis.

"There is a pattern to this, the cat was poisoned and then Bob Waldon and finally Kitty. Mrs Redford-Hamilton was probably experimenting with poisons and dosages to establish the correct dose. It's a pity we don't have her computer – she could have been searching for poisons on the internet, that would have given us some solid proof of her intentions."

The Deadend village was once more experiencing being headline news; reporters and television crews ascended on the village like vultures wanting any snippet of information and any morbid photographs and videos, they could get. The mood amongst the villagers was very sombre, Bob was well liked and to know his grave was being disturbed was most unsettling. The exhumation of old Bob Waldon's corpse was carried out behind a large screen, his coffin was transported into the town, and a forensic pathologist carried out the toxicology tests at the mortuary. The test results would be available to the police in a few weeks.

****

At The Old Vicarage, Ann and her husband had settled down for the evening in the lounge, to watch the television.

"I'm so cold," declared Ann. "I don't remember it being this cold in Canada!"

"It's the damp," replied Edward. "In Canada it's cold but dry and you don't feel the cold so much. Here, the cold and damp gets right into your bones. Also, this house isn't insulated like our place, it's so draughty."

"I wish we could go back to Canada, I miss the grandchildren terribly," Ann moaned.

"I'm the same, I don't like it here. I miss my ice fishing with my buddies. It won't be long now before they find bodies or something to give the police a lead."

"The body of that poor girl, just found, didn't help the police," Ann warily remarked. "Hilda couldn't just disappear into thin air without any clues. She messed up our lives when she was alive and now she's messing it up again when she is dead!" Ann exclaimed.

"We don't know she is dead until a body is found; we may have to wait till the courts declare her dead if no body turns up!"

"How long will that be?" Ann asked, fed up with the whole situation.

"It could be seven years!"

"Well I'm not waiting that long! I'll be packed and off home, long before then!" Ann replied angrily. Winston the cat jumped onto her lap and curled up. Ann stroked his warm furry coat contemplating on whether they should return to Canada soon.

They all sat, huddled near to the log fire. The lounge was a lot different from when they first saw it. The highly polished furniture was no longer shrouded in a film of dust, it reflected the light from the large bowl pendant light suspended from the ceiling and the table lamps, making the surfaces shine. Ann put another log from the basket onto the fire.

"Fred told me about the ice house in the field – in the old days they used to collect slabs of ice from the lake and store it together with their winter meat supply for the house; it was like their deep freeze. It's a work of art, you know, the ice house's domed shaped roof is made out of red bricks, then earth was piled on top leaving a small door to get in and out."

"Hey, she could be buried in there!" cried Ann excitedly.

"I doubt it, the cadaver dogs would have smelt any rotting flesh and besides the roof has partly collapsed – I went to see it with Fred yesterday."

"Where do you think a person would bury someone around here?" asked Ann, wanting to know immediate answers to solve the problem.

"They could have taken her body out of the village and hundreds of miles away; it may never be found!"

Ann cried out, "Don't say we are going to be stuck here for ever, I can't bear the thought of that!"

****

Tuesday morning, the village hall was open.

"Are you coming to line dancing tonight?" asked Brenda, taking the postage stamps from Jill, who was standing behind the counter of the post office, in the village hall.

"Yes, I'll be there," she replied with a smile. Brenda turned to walk out of the door and bumped into Fiona who was looking very gloomy.

"What's up with you?" Brenda inquisitively asked.

"Tim Waldon has just been informed by the police that his dad was poisoned and it was most likely by that Mrs Redford-Hamilton giving him poisoned food she often took around to him! Tim just told me on the phone."

"Gosh, do you think any of the food she brought to the functions and at her house dos, was poisoned? Was she going to kill us all off and have the village to herself?"

"That's going a bit too far, no one has suffered any of the symptoms apart from Bob and Kitty," Fiona replied.

"You forget, after her charity coffee morning, the first autumn she moved in, half the people that attended, suffered vomiting!"

Fiona thought back to that time, "Yes, and there was a vomiting bug going around most of the area at the time, towns and villages were affected and they didn't all come to the coffee morning, did they!"

"Mmm, it probably gave her the idea though!" Brenda retorted.

HILDA'S DAUGHTER IS FOUND

The two main detectives at the police station were having a general discussion about the Deadend village case.

"We can eliminate Irene, Kitty's daughter, from our inquiries, she didn't murder Mrs Redford-Hamilton, or Ann and Edward from Canada. Bob Waldon was the first poisoned victim of Hilda with that cherry mousse; it seems as if it was her trademark, Kitty was also given it – Tim Waldon can now be eliminated as a suspect," the lead detective stated, updating the junior detective.

He was reading the evidence board and replied: "So, we go back to the original list of suspects – the people who were blackmailed by Mrs Redford-Hamilton and possibly Steve Mann but we don't have a motive for him. We only have the suspicion, as he had done a runner."

"Steve Mann probably just ran because Carla Robinson is pregnant by him and she was only 15 at the time. Have the police in Cornwall caught up with him yet?"

His colleague replied, "No, he's a slippery customer, he's managing to stay one step ahead of them at the moment."

"So, we have three women, all appear to have disappeared on the same day, 29th August 2018 from the same village. Christine Holmes was found in the lake in her white car. Where are the other two?" He was thinking aloud. "If they are dead, which is highly likely, then where are their bodies and the items that were stolen from The Old Vicarage?"

"They could be anywhere," replied the other detective.

A police officer rushed in, disturbing their train of thought. "I think I've found Mrs Redford-Hamilton's daughter, Sir."

"Go on," the lead detective encouraged.

"Well, she changed her name by deed poll in Coventry when she was 21 years of age, from Elizabeth Charlotte Dudley-Fairfax to Lotty Dudley. It took me ages to find her because she took her partner's surname, Sanders, Lotty Sanders, but it wasn't by deed poll or by marriage! She wasn't paying National Insurance contributions either to make the search for her any easier."

"She's Mrs Redford-Hamilton's cleaner!" cried the lead detective. "She certainly had opportunity and motive; she hated her mother. I know Hilda usually paid everyone with cash so Lotty didn't need to pay her National Insurance."

"Why didn't her mother recognise her?" asked the police officer.

"Lotty left home when she was 16 years old, she will have changed a lot since then, she must be about 45 years old by now. We'll go and talk to her, see what she has to say for herself," the lead detective replied. He was smiling, he was pleased there was some breakthrough in the case at long last.

Lotty heard the knock at her front door at 2 Fell Road Cottages. She was surprised to open the door and find two detectives stood on the doorstep.

"We have a few questions for you, do you mind if we came in, to talk to you?"

"No, come through to the sitting room," Lotty nervously replied.

As they entered, Lotty introduced the man in the room, who had scrambled to his feet – "My partner, Cliff Sanders, please all take a seat." Cliff was about six feet in height, well built with sandy coloured hair; he was wearing overalls. The two detectives introduced themselves.

"I noticed you introduced your partner as Cliff Sanders when we came in, you also have the surname Sanders, is that your real name?" asked the leading detective to the reserved Lotty.

"No, my real name is Dudley – Lotty Dudley," she replied, wondering what they were there for.

"What name were you given at birth?" asked the lead detective coming straight to the point.

"Elizabeth… er," Lotty murmured very confused and embarrassed that she didn't know.

"I may be able to help you there," interrupted Cliff. "Lotty has had several nervous breakdowns and has lost a lot of her childhood memories and beyond, perhaps that's why she's confused."

"How old was she when you met her?"

"She was about 22 years of age, she was living on the streets in Coventry, she told me she had just lost her job and could no longer afford rent or food. I took pity on her; she was a beautiful girl and well spoken. I didn't want her picked up by a pimp and forced into prostitution, so I took her back to my house. She was unable to give me much information about her past. I believed she could have been very traumatised."

"What did she tell you? It doesn't matter how small the details," the lead detective kindly asked. He wanted to make sure she was definitely Hilda's daughter.

"Lotty knew she'd once lived in a grand house in London and had a very loving father. Her mother was cruel to her and sent her away to boarding school when her father died, she was very unhappy there, she was constantly bullied by the other girls."

Lotty began to cry at the glimpses of memories she could still recall from that time. Cliff warmly encircled his arms around her to comfort her.

"Lotty told me – she left home at 16 and worked in a care home, she also lodged there. When she turned 21, she changed her name by deed poll. Unfortunately, she lost her job the following year, she'd had a nervous breakdown and couldn't work, she hadn't seen a doctor and the care home staff didn't recognise her symptoms and just thought she was being lazy."

Lotty wiped the tears away from her eyes.

"That's when I met her, she's been with me ever since, we've had a child together, Annie, she's 21 this year." Cliff beamed a smile at Lotty, he was very proud to have them both as part of his family.

"What was Lotty's name at birth?" repeated the detective.

"I don't know, all her papers were stolen with her luggage when she was on the street, I only knew her as Lotty Dudley."

The detectives looked at Lotty, she appeared to be a quiet, sensitive person, it wasn't very likely she could have killed Mrs Redford-Hamilton or anyone else.

"Do you remember anything at all, Lotty, about your parents?" asked the lead detective in a gentle, encouraging voice.

"I was brought up by a nanny but I loved my father, he was gentle, kind and a very loving, white haired man. He gave me a beautiful doll with golden coloured hair on my 8th Birthday, I had lots of toys but this doll was extra special."

Lotty's eyes lit up at the wonderful memory she still had, of seeing the doll for the first time when she had opened her present.

"My mother never had any time for me, I didn't see her much but when I did, she was always shouting at me and punishing me for something or other. When my father died, my mother threw away all my toys and my precious doll, I had named her Annie. I was devastated! My mother told me 'to grow up'; she sent me away to boarding school. I was so alone and miserable, I hated being bullied." Lotty became emotional and began to cry again. Cliff sympathetically handed her his handkerchief and gave her a warm hug.

"I've been having flashbacks of little memories but there is one thing that stands out, it's this reoccurring nightmare I've had for ages; it's so very vivid, it terrifies me, I wake up screaming. I wonder if it's something to do with what I saw in my childhood."

"Please go on, explain it the best way you can," the detective asked her in a soft, gentle voice.

Nervously she continued – "I'm a little girl in my nightmare, I'm on a landing looking through the wooden railings, I'm crouched down. I see a woman and a man shouting at the top of the stairs. I'm frightened by their screams and noise and wonder if I should go back to my bedroom. I then see the woman push the man down the stairs – then I wake up screaming."

Both detectives glanced at each other thinking that maybe what she was reliving through her nightmares, were her own mother and father quarrelling and her mother, Mrs Hilda Redford-Hamilton, pushing her father downstairs, killing him.

Ann, Hilda's cousin from Canada, had told them her father had fallen downstairs and had broken his neck. It would have traumatized the little girl and on top of that, she had suffered her mother's cruelty as well as the bullying at the boarding school. It wasn't any wonder she had blocked a lot of her horrendous past out of her memory.

"Can you remember anything else about your mother?" asked the detective.

"She had a black mole just above her lip, she always wore a lot of jewellery and makeup. She always smelt really nice, probably her perfume. She wore lovely clothes and she could drive; she sometimes drove me back to boarding school."

"What name did your father call her?"

"He called her poppet, I remember this because my rag doll was also called poppet, he sometimes called me poppet too."

"Do you know if that was her real name?"

"No, I don't think it was my mother's real name, I can't remember what she was called, I called her Mummy and my father Papa. I didn't see my parents together very often as I was mostly with my nanny upstairs in the nursery. When I was older, I had a governess as well."

"Why did you leave your mother?"

"I hated her; she wouldn't let me do anything unless she was there – like going out with my friends. She repeatedly told me I was weak, she wouldn't let me attend any of her parties, she said I would 'let the side down!'. I had to leave home to get a life!"

"Did your mother remarry?"

"Yes, I think so, but I was at boarding school and hardly ever saw her new husband. When I came home from boarding school for the holidays, I was taken to the house I'd always lived in; my mother lived in another house. I was looked after by the housekeeper."

"What happened to the new husband?"

"He just wasn't around any longer, I didn't ask questions," Lotty replied, straining to remember any details.

"How old were you when he seemed to go out of your life?"

"A couple of years before I left, I think, probably when I was about 14 years of age."

"We know who your mother is," the lead detective suddenly informed her. Lotty looked shocked; she was stunned into silence. Cliff gasped in surprise.

"You have worked for her at The Old Vicarage, she's Mrs Hilda Redford-Hamilton."

Lotty and Cliff looked at each other, their mouths gaping with the shock and disbelief.

"She can't be my mother, she looked so different, spoke differently and didn't have the black mole above her lip, also my mother had straight hair!" cried Lotty in dismay.

"She had a lot of plastic surgery, tummy tucks and breast implants. She also wears wigs which could explain why she was so different. Your voice can alter living in different areas, picking up some of the local dialect. How did she treat you? Did she know who you were?"

"She just treated me like a cleaner, she didn't tell me anything about her life and wasn't interested in mine. She was always waiting for me, she expected me to be there on the dot for work. Each room I cleaned she would be there doing something as if she was keeping an eye on me all the time. There were certain rooms I was forbidden to enter."

"What rooms were they?"

"The room next to her bedroom."

The detective realized it was her mother's dressing room where she stored her expensive clothes and jewellery. Perhaps she didn't trust Lotty going in there. It was where her mother had her binoculars, by the window overlooking the graveyard.

Lotty continued, "Also she forbade me to go anywhere near the wooden stairs leading to the attic."

The detectives wondered if there was some significance in that.

"So, you never suspected it was your mother, not even from the painting of her hung up in the dining room, over the fireplace?"

"No, I would never have dreamt that my mother would choose to live in a remote village in the north of England and leave her flamboyant lifestyle with the rich and famous behind her in London, it just wasn't her! Besides she didn't have the mole or even look at all like my mother. The painting didn't 'ring any bells' at all, it just didn't look like her." Lotty was becoming upset, she thought she was being accused of something to do with her mother's disappearance.

"We are not accusing you of anything, we just want to know every detail to eliminate you from our inquiries."

Cliff spoke up. "If we knew Mrs Redford-Hamilton was her mother we would have moved, Lotty would never have wanted to work for her as a cleaner. I'm sure Mrs Redford-Hamilton didn't recognize Lotty or she would have said something to her."

The detectives tended to agree.

"On Wednesday, 29th August 2018, you left work at 12 noon. Was there anything out of the ordinary that day, did she appear normal to you?"

"It was just a normal day at work, if anything she appeared to be in a cheerful mood," Lotty explained.

"Did she say she was going anywhere that day?" the younger detective asked.

"No, but she usually didn't say anything about her private life, any way!"

"What was she wearing?"

"It was summer so she would've been wearing a dress and a cardigan; if she went to the town, she would wear a summer jacket and a hat. She would always take a summer handbag, she was very particular that it matched her hat and shoes."

"Do you know Ann Harrison and her husband Edward Harrison, who have arrived from Canada and are tidying up The Old Vicarage?" the lead detective asked, watching Lotty's body language for any clues; they didn't know she actually worked for them.

"Yes, they asked me to clean for them," she answered, surprised the couple had been mentioned.

"Ann is your mother's cousin," the other detective informed her. Both Cliff and Lotty looked at each other astounded.

"So, you didn't know she was related to you?" asked the lead detective.

"No," they both replied in unison.

"Did you know of them in your youth, Lotty?"

"All I remember is – I had an auntie and uncle, their affectionate names were, Auntie Annie and Uncle Eddie, I used to write to Auntie Annie but I only met them once before my father died. She often wrote very kind and loving letters to me. I remembered her name as I named my doll after her because she was so caring. Is it really them?"

"Yes, it is, didn't you recognize your auntie or uncle at all?"

"No, they are a lot older now, it must have been about... 38 years ago since I last saw them, they speak with a strong

Canadian accent now." Lotty was still very shocked that she had relatives in the same remote village!

"We have taken up a lot of your time this evening, thank you for your help; we will not require any more interviews from you. We are going to call on The Old Vicarage on our way out – should we let them know who you are?"

"Oh yes, yes please, they will be as shocked as we are about who I am," cried Lotty.

When the detectives left, Cliff and Lotty sat on the settee, staring at each other in silence for a few moments. All the information they had learnt was a lot to process.

"You'll have to see Ann and Edward, they will be so excited now you are a relative of theirs," uttered Cliff. His eyes were twinkling with excitement, he lovingly wrapped his arms around her slim body.

Lotty kissed his cheek. "I'm so grateful you took care of me and brought me here, or else I would never have discovered who I really am!"

Cliff gently took her hand and led her upstairs to the bedroom; they were both smiling and felt very happy. He kissed her so lovingly and guided her to the soft duvet and laid her down. Lotty looked into his romantic, mellow blue eyes and smiled. "I love you so much, you are everything to me."

Cliff affectionately caressed her, she cherished his little kisses down her slender neck and cheek, they sent waves of passion through her warm body; she felt so lucky.

Cliff gently undressed her and slipped out of his own clothes, their bare skin touched, they hugged each other tightly under the duvet. Both tenderly touched and caressed each other's warm, loving, sensual bodies with deep affection. Their kisses were tender on their warm, moist lips – with arousing passions stirring like the young love they had once known; they reached the crescendo of absolute ecstasy. Pulses were high and cheeks were flushed as they slid back to rest side by side; they fell into a deep and peaceful sleep.

****

The two detectives had driven down the village that night, the bright full moon lit the dark sky and reflected on the wet road. They stopped at The Old Vicarage on their way home. They wanted to corroborate Lotty's story, that neither parties – Lotty, Cliff and Ann and Edward – knew each other, to quash the idea that they all had something to do with Mrs Redford-Hamilton's disappearance.

Ann invited them into the lounge; she knew they would have completed their investigations, about her and her husband regarding Mrs Redford-Hamilton's will.

"We have eliminated you from our investigations, Mrs Redford-Hamilton's will was found to be genuine, here is the original copy," the leading detective announced, passing over the document in the brown envelope. Ann smiled; she was relieved she was no longer a suspect.

"When will you be returning home to Canada?" Ann was asked.

"We don't know, we can hardly leave this place with all the precious items stored here, they may be stolen! There's also Winston to take care of. We would also like to see Hilda return and tells us where the hell she's been! Or the case to be resolved one way or another!" Ann exclaimed, a bit annoyed.

"We would like to ask when you last saw Elizabeth Charlotte Dudley-Fairfax, Mrs Redford-Hamilton's only daughter by her first marriage," the lead detective suddenly asked.

Ann and Edward looked at each other trying to calculate when they had last encountered her. Edward responded, "Wasn't it before her father died? We never met her step-father."

"Yes, I believe you're right, perhaps when she was about seven years old, we came back from Canada on a visit to England and called in."

The lead detective suddenly announced – "We have found Elizabeth."

Ann and Edward looked shocked and feared the worst, it flashed through both of their minds that they had found her body somewhere.

"Do you mean she's dead?" asked Ann shocked and afraid; she had cupped her hands around her mouth and nose in consternation.

The lead detective continued – "No, she is not dead, she is very much alive!" Both Ann and Edward sighed with relief and grinned at each other.

"She has changed her name; she is now known as Lotty Sanders!" the lead detective exclaimed with a smile.

Ann and Edward glanced at each other they were totally astounded and gasped in surprise.

"You mean Lotty, who cleans for us?" Ann asked, not believing what she was hearing.

"Yes, it's Elizabeth, I'll leave her to fill in the gaps in her life for you, we have just come from her house."

Both Ann and Edward looked at each other with a beaming smile, they hugged each other. "We've found her at last, this is wonderful news, we can't thank you enough." Ann laughed gleefully. She then asked, "How are you coming on with your investigation about my cousin Hilda, are you any nearer to finding her?"

"We are in the process of tracking down a possible witness to her disappearance," the lead detective informed her.

The detectives left to return to the police station. The detectives were pleased that they were able to give someone some good news for a change from their investigations. They were convinced the two parties didn't know who each other were. The police detectives eliminated any suggestion that they were involved in Mrs Redford-Hamilton's disappearance.

Ann cried out in an extremely enthusiast voice, "We'll quickly go around to Lotty's house now, oh, what wonderful news, she is alive and lives in the village!"

"It's a bit late, leave it till tomorrow, she'll be coming to work in the morning," Edward advised her.

The following morning, Ann and Edward waited patiently for Lotty to arrive for work; they were busting with happiness. Lotty was very excited herself to be meeting the only surviving family she had. She eagerly knocked on the back door and Ann immediately opened it and without a word gave her a big hug, Lotty was exuberant that she had found her loving Auntie Annie. Edward joined in the joyous hugs and kisses, tears ran down their cheeks, their long-lost relative had been found at last.

"You're not working today, love," Ann joyously announced to Lotty in an emotional voice. "Come and sit in the lounge, I'll make us all a cup of tea."

"We've got a lot of years to catch up on!" joined in Edward, laughing.

Lotty took a seat next to Ann. "I named my precious doll after you, you know – she was called Annie, I always called you Auntie Annie and you, Uncle Eddie. I've remembered that much. There are some things I can't remember, there are big blanks in my life."

"We always called you Lizzie," Ann replied, placing a loving arm around her.

"I don't recollect that," Lotty answered, trying desperately to remember through the fog in her memory.

"Your mother was disgusted at us calling you Lizzie, she hated names shortened or changed in any way." Ann laughed, wiping away the tears that were still welling up in her eyes.

"Well, tell us about your life adventures up till now, what has happened to you in all these years?" Ann asked, bursting with enthusiasm.

"I'm afraid it's a very traumatic period in my life until I met my partner Cliff, he saved me!" Lotty began to tell her sorrowful story, and there wasn't a dry eye between them. Ann knew she didn't get on with her mother but was angry at the cruelty Lotty endured after her father died when she was only eight.

"I was often locked in the cupboard, it was pitch black, I hated the dark, I was absolutely terrified. Some nights I went to bed and cried all night, I was desperately unhappy."

Ann wept when she heard Lotty had lived on the streets, she knew her mother had deprived Lotty of her rightful inheritance from her beloved father.

"When I met Cliff, my life totally changed! He is so loving and caring, he looked after me like no other person has, he was always there for me. We wanted to get married but couldn't afford to, he had taken a lot of time off work to look after me and he had lost his job because of it. He eventually became a self-employed builder and joiner, I'm so proud of him. We have a daughter Annie named after you as well, she will be 21 this summer."

Ann's face creased into a large grin but underneath she was overwhelmed emotionally.

"We'll have to make it a very special occasion, the 21st birthday party with a big family reunion!" Edward suggested.

"That would be wonderful." Lotty hugged her kind Uncle Eddie. "Annie works in the town, she is a staff nurse at the hospital," Lotty told them, feeling deeply proud of her.

"We would love to meet her," Ann replied, very excited. "Why didn't you write to me, dear, when you knew you would have to go on the streets to live? We would have looked after you," Ann asked Lotty, giving her a big hug on the settee where they sat.

Lotty told them – "When my mother threw away my toys, she didn't stop there, in later years, she threw away all my diaries and my address book. I couldn't remember your address because you had recently moved from Alberta to somewhere else in Canada."

"Oh, you poor dear, you must have felt utterly destitute and afraid." Tears were streaming down Ann's cheeks; Edward was trying hard to fight back his own tears.

After Lotty had left, Edward asked, "Why didn't you mention Hilda's will?"

Ann looked at him, "I didn't want to upset her even more about her mother, it was Hilda's final nail in poor Lotty's coffin to finally disown her and deprive her of her inheritance. There will be plenty of other times to tell her."

Edward pondered for a while and continued, "Well, if it was me, I'd let Lotty have what's rightfully hers."

"You're absolutely right, Lotty should get everything not me, I was only Hilda's cousin after all. Besides, the money was made by Lotty's father, Hilda never made a penny of it! She just spent it, frittering it away as though there was no tomorrow." Ann sighed. "I should change my will, so if I do inherit Hilda's estate then die suddenly, Lotty will get what's rightfully hers."

****

The police arrived at The Old Vicarage, the following day. They had been sent to search the attic again, as Mrs Redford-Hamilton had not allowed Lotty to go into the attic for some reason. It was a long shot but they were desperate for any more leads.

"Would you mind if we searched the attic again? There has been a possible new lead," the polite police officer asked Ann at the door.

"Come in, you are welcome to search where you like, we want this investigation finished as much as you do."

The two police officers, Edward and Ann climbed the wooden stairs into the attic. Torches where switched on, to scan the two rooms. All four of them diligently searched every inch.

"What exactly are we looking for?" Edward asked, becoming despondent at not finding anything.

"Anything really," came the reply.

Edward scrutinized the stone fireplace – he noticed one of the stones was not secured with mortar and he gently eased it out.

"Look, there's something here!" he gasped. One of the officers managed to retrieve the item from the hole in the wall of the fireplace, with his handkerchief. He inspected it and remarked – "It could be a bottle of poison, we will have it analysed."

"It's a modern bottle, it can't have been left from times gone by," Ann observed. They all carried on the search but nothing else was found.

STEVE MANN IS FOUND

Life in the village continued, the aggressive, determined newspaper reporters, television reporters and cameramen had dwindled away leaving the villagers in peace.

"Are you going to the music club tonight?" asked Fay. She was a good-looking woman in her 30s, dressed in jeans and layers of jumpers. Jean looked up from her pencil sketch of a bowl of fruit, she was finishing in the art class, in the village hall.

"Yes, I'll be there, I'll bring my banjo – what are you bringing?" Jean asked. Fay placed her large sketch pad in her carrier bag and replied, "I'll bring my guitar, I'll walk you home, if you like, I'm calling in on my sister."

"Bye, ladies, both your work is improving, you are doing very well, see you next week," Craig Ruddy called after them. They both waved goodbye.

Outside in the cool air they strode quickly up the village road to keep warm. Jean was older, she was in her 40s, she was warmly dressed in a padded coat, woolly hat and fur lined boots.

"Have you heard? Lotty is related to the old couple staying at The Old Vicarage," Jean asked Fay, who was muffled up in a long white scarf wound around her neck several times.

"She'll be related to Mrs H.R.H. then because the Canadian couple there are cousins of Mrs H.R.H., thank goodness Lotty's not a bit like Mrs H.R.H.!" Fay exclaimed. They stood and talked for a while.

"I didn't like Mrs Redford-Hamilton, she was so nasty to poor old Ada. Do you remember at that meeting when Ada plucked up the courage to join us after shutting herself away, mourning her husband for weeks? She had brought her old dog to give her confidence. Mrs H.R.H. shouted at her, in that booming voice of hers, from the front of the hall to the back, 'get that smelly dirty mutt out of here!' Poor Ada burst into tears and left; half the hall of people emptied in sympathy for Ada. Then Mrs H.R.H. had the audacity to ask, 'why is everyone leaving? It's ridiculous!' – Stupid woman, she has no empathy for anyone, I've no time for her."

Fay told her she wasn't there to witness it.

"I've been invited to a wife swapping party next week at Ibby's house!" Fay continued excitedly. "Don't tell anyone, will you," laughed Fay mischievously.

"Oh, gosh! What do you do exactly? Wasn't all that the rage with swingers in the 60s and 70s?" Jean curiously asked – she wanted to know all the explicit details.

Fay continued: "Yes, I think it was but before my time!" She paused, fumbling in her pocket for a tissue, the cold was making her 'nose run'. "Well, we start off with a party, plenty of alcohol and finger food, to get us in the mooood! When everyone is ready, the fellas throw their car keys in a bowl, their wives pick a key out and you are paired with whoever owns the key."

"Then what?" Jean asked, pushing for more answers.

"Well, you all disperse into separate rooms, at some parties you go home with them, then it's up to you what you do, if you want to go all the way or just kiss and cuddle," Fay answered giggling.

"What happens if you don't like the man you're paired up with?" asked Jean, not liking at all what she was hearing.

"I suppose you could just talk all evening, it would be pretty boring though," Fay replied sniggering.

"Sounds to me, it's a playground for starting affairs and babies, splitting marriages and getting diseases!" Jean replied most indignant.

"You're such a prude, Jean, my husband and I get a kick out of an open relationship; we enjoy living life to the full, live and let live – I say, it'll be great fun!" Fay retorted.

Jean answered back, "I believe in the sanctity of marriage. I love my husband and would never be unfaithful to him. I wouldn't want another man!"

"Well, I'm not going to lose your friendship over this, we will have to agree to disagree," Fay announced; she didn't want to lose a good friend. They both bid goodnight and went their separate ways.

****

Ann and Edward had invited Lotty around for lunch at The Old Vicarage. Ann cheerfully invited her in through the open front door. "Come in, love, it's wonderful to see you again."

"I haven't had a decent night's sleep since I found out you are my Auntie Annie and Uncle Eddie and all about my horrid mother, it's been spinning around my head all the time!" Lotty replied, grinning from ear to ear as she took off her outdoor clothes.

"We would like to tell you a few more details, so perhaps tonight you'll not sleep either!" Ann grinned to let Lotty know it wasn't going to be bad news.

Lotty lay her gloves on the hall table and followed her Uncle Eddie and Auntie Annie into the lounge.

"We have found Hilda's will – your mother's will," Ann excitedly told Lotty. "Unfortunately, she has cut you out of her will, but don't worry because we will give you what is rightfully yours."

"I don't understand, how can you do that?" asked Lotty very confused.

Edward tried to clarify Ann's bundled attempt to explain. "She is trying to tell you that she is the sole beneficiary to your mother's will and she is going to gift everything to you! That's when she inherits it, of course!"

Ann laughed. "Just think, you will be able to make this house into a care home like you wished!"

"But the police are not absolutely certain my mother is dead, there has been no body found!" Lotty cried out in alarm.

"Her body will be found soon, I know it. She hasn't left willingly, she wouldn't have left her cat Winston, now would she? You were destined to inherit what's rightfully yours. We will leave and return to Canada soon; you can look after the place until the investigations are over."

Lotty was overwhelmed and upset. "I don't want you to leave, I've only just found you! And I don't have the money to run this place or pay the gardener!"

"Don't worry, Lotty, we will come and visit you often; we will be here for your daughter's 21st birthday party in the summer with our family, so you can get to know them. We have seen your mother's solicitor and money has been arranged to pay you and Fred to keep the place going. Your mother, for once, was very astute at arranging an account with her solicitor for emergencies. I've changed my will so if I die suddenly after inheriting your mother's estate, you will get what's rightfully yours! As soon as I can I'll gift your mother's estate to you."

"Oh, thank you, thank you Auntie Annie, I can't wait to tell Cliff when he comes home tonight. He will be so shocked!"

"I understand that you have never been in the dressing room or the attic. I'll show you around after lunch, if you like?" Ann grinned and lightly held Lotty's hand.

Lotty was still in deep shock, she was still trying to comprehend everything she had been told. After lunch in the kitchen, Ann showed Lotty into the dressing room and showed her the gowns, clothes and jewellery.

Lotty gasped. "My memory is coming back; I recognize some of these! I particularly remember this bracelet as I accidentally broke it, it caught on my fluffy woollen jumper when my mother brushed past me, it flew apart! My mother slapped me across the face for breaking it… it looks as if she's repaired it." They all ascended the wooden steps to the attic.

"You could make this into a self-contained flat for you and your partner, I'm sure Cliff has the skills to make it into a lovely apartment," Ann suggested. "You'll need to sell your mother's clothes and jewellery to finance the project, a lift will need to be installed downstairs and more en-suite bathrooms put in the bedrooms ready for your care home."

Lotty smiled; she thought her Auntie Annie was 'jumping the gun' a bit as her mother hadn't even been found.

"I'll help you photograph and catalogue all your mother's items in the dressing room, ready for auction before I return to Canada," Ann had offered, trying to be helpful.

When Lotty left the house, her head was in a spin from all the information whirling around. She began planning the apartment in the attic in her mind. She was ecstatically happy and felt a little guilty that she wasn't even upset about her mother's disappearance.

****

It was a lovely bright sunny day but cool, families were dressed in their Sunday best and strolled down the road to the village church. It was Mothering Sunday.

"I'm so grateful we have such a young dynamic vicar, he has brought us into the modern era," Carol remarked to Jenny.

"His grandfather was the same, he did a tremendous amount of work for the community, he was a very forward thinker for his time," Jenny replied, admiring the blaze of colour from the yellow daffodils growing on the grass verges. The daffodil's vibrant trumpet like corona blooms fluttered in the breeze, appearing to trumpet out their calls to be noticed.

In the middle of the service, the children were invited to the front of the church to the chancel, the area around the altar. Large wicker baskets held small bunches of daffodils tied with a yellow ribbon into a bow.

The little excited children, wide eyed, beamed smiles as they were presented one by one with the flowers to give to their waiting mothers, sitting patiently in the pews. Some of the children hugged and kissed their mothers, others showed a little embarrassment and just handed the bundles of flowers over, unceremoniously. When the service was over, the vicar stood at the main door, as the congregation filed past, smiling and thanking him for the lovely service.

"He is so well liked," someone uttered as the crowd of people walked towards the church gates.

"Yes, he is well loved, not like Mrs Redford-Hamilton, she is the most hated person I know," replied another.

"The police are no nearer to finding her, I heard they found a bottle of poison in her attic with her fingerprints on it, I don't know if that was just a rumour but we know she poisoned Gail's cat, Old Bob and poor Kitty."

"I believe it has definitely been confirmed about the poison in the bottle, apparently it was a cocktail of poisons. The bottle only had her fingerprints on, no one else's prints. The police had compared the fingerprints taken off the bottle, to the prints obtained some time ago from her hairbrush – they were a match."

Jenny was walking past the women, and on overhearing their conversation, she exclaimed –

"She is a vile, evil woman, she'd better not come back here, there's enough anger and hate in this village that she could be lynched!"

"If she does come back, she will definitely be arrested and sent to prison, I wonder how they will manage her in there!" exclaimed another woman.

They all laughed out loud, it was hard to imagine the haughty, arrogant Mrs Redford-Hamilton conforming to other authorities' rules and regulations.

****

The following Friday, a police officer rushed into the leading detective's office at the police station.

"Sir, a bell rope has been found about 20 miles away, a dog had pulled part of it from the mud. The owner of the dog pulled the rest of it out, it has a blue and yellow sally, the same colours as the bell ropes in Deadend village church!"

"This is what we have been waiting for, it could be a good lead, perhaps we will find a body there as well," the senior detective replied, grabbing his coat from the coat stand and taking the piece of paper from the police officer's hand. He read the location of the incident and travelled to the site with a group of police officers.

It was an isolated area, about a mile from the main road, up a muddy single-track road. The police observed the caller who had rung in on his mobile phone. The man was obviously a keen walker judging by the clothes and footwear he was wearing; he was stood waiting patiently for them with his dog. He immediately showed the police where they had found the rope in the sticky mud. The site was wasteland, dotted with a few trees, gorse bushes and patches of coarse grass. No one would have seen a vehicle there from the road, or anyone trying to bury a rope or a body.

"It was lucky your dog found it, what breed is he?" the leading detective asked, grateful for a lead in the case.

The man smiled and looked at his faithful companion and replied, "He's a labradoodle, I've had him since he was a pup."

The area was cordoned off, the muddy bell rope was bagged and tagged for evidence. The policemen dug down with spades to see if a body was buried beneath, but they were hampered by the heavy, viscous, tacky mud. They dug down deep, their wellington boots and clothes got clarted in mud but they found nothing for all their sweat and hard work.

"I'll arrange for cadaver dogs to sniff the area, see if they can pick up the scent of any human remains."

The cadaver dogs arrived, they piled out of the police van wagging their tails, eager to do their work. The dog handlers took their dogs to different parts of the large area of wasteland, and an intensive search of the ground ensued. As time went by, doubts grew of finding a corpse or any remains, the light was fading, it was time to abandon all hopes of finding anymore leads.

****

At The Old Vicarage Ann and Edward were entertaining Lotty, her partner Cliff and their daughter Annie. They were dining in the grand dining room in style! The table was set with the solid silver cutlery, the table was adorned with the two large silver peacocks from the dresser to make a centrepiece for the table.

"Annie," Ann began after the first course was eaten, "your mother was brought up to be a lady, you know." Annie chuckled; she had only known her mother, Lotty, to be a hard worker, they had lived fairly simply as she was growing up.

Lotty laughed. "I went from grandeur to the streets!"

"Yes, from riches to rags!" Cliff exclaimed.

"What was Mrs Redford-Hamilton like, or I should say my grandmother," asked Annie curious about the regal lady in the painting, hung over the fireplace.

Ann enlightened her about her grandmother's youth and how she had married a rich older man – her grandfather – and the many lessons and presents showered upon her to the time Lotty was born.

Annie replied, "So she was just as ordinary as we are then, only she was a social climber that got lucky. Why would she come to a place like this when she had a fabulous life in London?"

Ann again tried to enlighten her. "When your grandfather fell down the stairs and broke his neck—"

Lotty gasped. "Did he fall down the stairs!" she asked in disbelief.

Ann looked over to her across the table.

"Yes, didn't you know, dear, I'm sorry but yes he did."

Lotty was shocked. "That explains the years and years of a recurring nightmare I've had, I'm in my nightie crouched on the landing, looking through the banister railings. I'm watching a man and woman arguing–" Lotty began to cry; through her tears she tells them she saw the woman push the man down the stairs.

"Oh, my poor dear, you could have witnessed your beloved father being murdered by your horrible mother!" Ann cried out. She rushed around the table to give Lotty a big hug. When Lotty regained her composure, Ann continued with her story about Lotty's mother.

"After her second rich husband died from a fall while out walking–"

Lotty interrupted her again. "Was my mother walking with him?"

"Yes, I'm afraid she was, he fell down a steep slope and hit his head on a rock and died. The police had no evidence to suggest either death was suspicious."

Lotty and her daughter Annie both gasped with the realization that it was possible both deaths were intended murder.

Ann continued her story:

"She was shunned in high society, she was nicknamed 'the black widow'. She knew she wouldn't find another rich man, although she did try by going on expensive cruises. Finally, she decided to come here and play the part of 'the lady of the manor', so I'm afraid that is the sorry tale of your grandmother," Ann explained to Annie.

"I will never forgive her for killing my father, he was so loving to me, how could she do such a thing!" Lotty cried out.

"He was a lot older than her. Once he had taught her to be a high society lady, she had no use for him, she only wanted his money; same with her second husband."

"I hope my mother is dead, she doesn't deserve to live," screamed Lotty. Cliff lovingly held her hand to comfort her and help calm her down.

"I think the villagers have done away with her somehow, they hated her and those other women just happened to come across the event and witnessed what was going on. Christine Holmes probably escaped but careered off the road," Ann surmised.

"That's just pure speculation, Ann, we should wait for the police to finish their investigation before jumping to conclusions," her husband coolly remarked.

"I'm not surprised the villagers hate her," began Lotty. "I remember the cat being poisoned and the owners blamed my mother, then Old Bob died after she was delivering cherry mousse to him, his favourite dessert. Cherry mousse was also delivered to Kitty's house by my mother too; fortunately, Kitty didn't like it. But Kitty fell ill eating the other food she took to her. It's a good job my mother disappeared when she did or Kitty could have been poisoned to death as well! The police have all the proof apart from the poisoning of the cat. I hate calling her my mother, from now on I will call her Mrs Redford-Hamilton, I totally disown her... What was my grandmother like?"

"Your grandmother and grandfather died in a train crash when Hilda was three, I was only eight at the time. I only met them a few times as they lived in Yorkshire, they were a well-respected, hardworking couple, both worked in the woollen industry in the mills."

"Where did Hilda get her desire to be something she wasn't?" Annie asked, not daring to mention the word 'grandmother', so as not to upset her mother Lotty.

"Well, whether it was the fact she was an orphan and wanted to be somebody or that her parents spoilt her I don't know. But she was always a strange child, she had no empathy for animals and birds – I told the police she used to shoot sparrows and cats if they got on our lawn. I had a beautiful smoky blue-haired cat, she had four beautiful kittens. Hilda was quite young at the time but the little evil devil cut off their tails with a pair of scissors!"

Lotty and Annie gasped in astonishment.

"The poor innocent creatures; she must have been mentally sick to do something as horrific as that," Lotty cried out.

"She got a walloping from my dad for that!" Ann remembered. "Thank goodness you both didn't turn out like her, one in the family is more than enough. Now, would anyone like a dessert? There's no cherry mousse I'm afraid."

They all laughed, the intense atmosphere surrounding their conversation had dissipated. The large, empty bone china dinner plates and the solid silver cutlery were removed to the kitchen.

"We better not put these in the dish washer," Ann muttered to Lotty. Ann laughed. "It's nice to dress up and occasionally have a meal like this but I wouldn't want the palaver every day."

The desserts were carried through to the dining room. Cliff was telling jokes, making everyone laugh. The dinner party ended in a happy success, and Ann was pleased with herself, she knew she was blessed to have such wonderful relatives.

They had coffee and mints in the lavish drawing room. Lotty had remembered the black cobweb that had straddled the paintings – the room was sparkling now after its thorough clean.

"Can you still remember how to play the piano, Lotty? You had lessons when you were younger, do you remember?" Ann asked.

"It's years since I played the piano! It must have been when I was at boarding school." Lotty lifted the fallboard and began to play a simple tune. They all clapped; it was wonderful to bring life and merriment to the old house, as a family.

Edward announced, "Ann and I will be leaving the day after tomorrow, we will keep in touch on our computer back in Canada, we want to know everything that goes on about the police investigations. Particularly about Hilda."

Lotty, Cliff and Annie would be sad to see them leave. Ann reassured Lotty she would send all the copies of photos about the family and of Lotty's young life, which may help her to remember her early years.

****

When the lead detective returned to his office after a meeting, his gloomy mood lightened. A call had been received from Cornwall. The police officer informed him: "They have found Steve Mann, he was taken in for questioning, he refuses to speak to the detectives there. He said he would 'only speak to the lead detective in the Deadend village case'. Should I inform them you are on your way? Sir."

"Yes, I'll travel down immediately," came the reply. He hurried to retrieve his file on the case. He collected an overnight bag from his house and set off to Cornwall with another police officer. They both felt the adrenaline pumping and hoped this was going to be a lucky break in the case.

****

At Deadend village, Betty and Gill were ambling down the village road to the village hall ready for the circle dancing that evening. During their conversation Betty told her:

"The elderly couple from Canada have left The Old Vicarage, Lotty is probably in charge of it now. It's doubtful Mrs Redford-Hamilton will return, it's been a long time since we all saw her."

"She's been murdered, I bet, I shan't miss her. Did you hear about Ibby's wife swapping party? She could only persuade Fay and her husband to go, out of the whole village; the other couples were drafted in from the town."

"I heard it was a very drunken, raucous party, Fay described it as hot, erotic, sexy and steamy! It's not my

145

sort of party, it sounds as if they were out of control!" Betty exclaimed.

"I wouldn't go to a party like that, I wonder if they were on drugs! I heard Jenny Kiln's young son was found with drugs at school, poor Jenny she must have been devastated. It's hard bringing up kids these days, what with drugs everywhere, cyber bullying on mobile phones, stress with body image and kids still have to cope with the constant testing and exams at school."

"What did the police do with Jenny's son? He would be only 14," Betty asked.

"He would probably have had a youth caution, but it will still go on his record, so he better behave himself from now on or he'll end up in court!"

"What's happening to our quiet way of life in Deadend village? Everything seems to have gone completely mad," Betty remarked, feeling down about the year's events. They entered the village hall and immediately went to stand by the radiator to warm themselves. Villagers trickled into the room in twos and threes, chatting and laughing. It was good for them to get together dancing and having a good laugh.

****

The following day, the detective left in charge of the case at the police station, was informed that the bell rope found in the mud by the dog had been forensically analysed. There were no traces of DNA on it. He decided he would wait for the return of the lead detective from Cornwall, before questioning the vicar about a possible missing bell rope from the bell tower. It could have been replaced as there were four bell ropes present when the search took place in the church.

A call came in from another police station, and the detective received the call. A badly decomposing body had been found that day, in a remote area. The items surrounding the remains were similar to what Cathy Reed was wearing and the rucksack she was carrying, on the day she was given a lift to the church in Deadend village.

"I'm on my way," replied the detective. At the scene, along a side road, down an overgrown embankment, was a crumpled-up body of a female amongst the brambles and bushes. The whole scene was investigated and photographed. What was left of the body was lifted into a black body bag and taken away for further forensic analysis. The items left were bagged and tagged for evidence.

Back at the police station, the lead detective had arrived back with Steve Mann, from Cornwall. They walked into the custody suite, Steve looked pale and drawn. He was of average height and walked with a stoop, his untidy blond hair partly covered his unshaven face, his square jaw with a cleft chin, were a prominent feature of his appearance. The lead detective presented Steve to the custody officer and explained the circumstances of his arrest. Steve was processed and held in custody in a cell. He was able to rest and have a meal before further questioning. He was relieved he was in custody – he had been running from something far more frightening than the police!

STEVE MANN'S STRANGE STORY

The bell ringers arrived at the bell tower, for practice. Little did they know a woman had been hanged there the previous year on 29th August 2018. Everyone went to their places by their small mats, numbered one to four. Mat 2 remained empty, it had been Mrs Redford-Hamilton's place, the self-appointed master bell ringer.

"I'm glad we don't have to put up with Mrs H.R.H. She was always picking on someone for not testing their bell when they had already done so," Mildred murmured as she set up her box to stand on, to give her some height. They all unhooked their bell ropes and tested their bells with the ends of their ropes – it was to make sure the bells were down and positioned safely. They heard hurried steps on the wooden steps outside the door.

"Sorry I'm late, I was delayed by a phone call," the young vicar explained. He hurried to stand on the vacant mat marked number 2. He didn't appear to have his mind on the job and Jenny had to gently remind him to test his bell. They all began to wrap the bell ropes in coils around their left hands, they placed their other hand on the blue and yellow sally, ready to begin. They were all smiles apart from the vicar who appeared to be in a daze.

Jake started on mat one. "Look to! treble going, treble gone," he told them, pulling down on his rope.

Mildred had told them they would ring rounds, so one after another they pulled on their bell ropes. The four blue and yellow sallies, one by one disappeared through holes in the ceiling as they let go of them. The bells loudly rang out in the belfry above, their clappers struck the inside of the bells vibrating the air with a lovely resonance.

Jenny remembered being shouted at by Mrs H.R.H. – 'Hold up at hand stroke you're clipping the second bell!' Jenny smiled, it was far more pleasant with the group they had now, she didn't feel so nervous.

Mildred, on mat 4, said, "Two to three." Jenny responded by ringing her bell before the vicar's bell number two. Jenny chuckled to herself remembering Mrs H.R.H., it seemed she was still stood to her right, shouting at her as she was looking at the wrong bell ringer to time her strokes. 'You should know by now what to do, you've been ringing long enough!' She could still hear that booming voice of hers, echoing in the room! Jenny felt she was picked on most weeks for something. The bell ringers had a rest and chattered about the weather.

Jake uttered, "It's lovely bell ringing without you know who!" They all laughed then began to ring their bells again, it was a pleasant, joyful, uplifting atmosphere with the sound of the bells pealing in the belfry. When they had finished after about half an hour, the bells were brought down with their bell ropes to rest in a safe position. The bell ropes were secured to the hooks on the discoloured white walls. They chatted as they walked down the wooden steps, apart from the vicar who was unusually quiet and had a frown on his forehead, as if he was deep in thought. These were the same steps, the middle aged Christine Holmes had ran down, terrified after seeing the body of a woman hanging from a bell rope! The bell ringers had opened the door and entered the church. They had walked out through the main door not knowing the awful trauma that had taken place that day.

"See you on Sunday at quarter to ten, everybody!" Jenny called out.

****

In the interview room at the police headquarters in the town, the lead detective wiped his black rimmed glasses with his handkerchief and asked Steve Mann, "Did you manage to rest and have a meal after our long journey?"

"Yes, I'm ready to talk," he replied, quite relaxed.

The detectives continued after the introductions had been made for the recording. "Have you ever been married, Mr Mann?"

"Yes, for 23 years to my dear wife, Letty. Sadly, she died of ovarian cancer about three years ago."

"Do you have any children?" he was asked.

"No, unfortunately my wife was unable to have children."

"Now we will start with your relationship with a minor, Carla Robinson. Did you know she was only 15 at the time you had under-age sex with her?"

"Yes, she told me her age when I first met her," Steve Mann replied as he crossed his legs.

"When did your relationship begin?" was the next question asked.

Steve thought for a while. "Possibly May last year, well, that was when I started taking her out shoeing horses and ponies, with me."

The lead detective asked for further clarification. "How did your relationship start?"

Steve shuffled in his seat. "I first met her when I went to shoe her new Arab pony, she was interested in me telling her about my job. I told her I travelled around the area shoeing ponies, horses and even racehorses."

"Then what happened?" asked the lead detective.

"She asked if she could go to the racing stables with me to shoe racehorses, she wanted to be a jockey. So, I told her the next time I went there, I would pick her up, with her parents' permission of course."

"Please continue," the detective encouraged him.

Steve brushed his blond hair off his face with his hand.

"She began coming with me on other occasions, I noticed she was starting to dress up for our days out shoeing, you know, tank tops, tight leggings, makeup and false eye lashes. She even had false nails on sometimes. I remembered her lovely long curly auburn hair flowed onto her slim shoulders. We would sit in the Land Rover for lunch and eat our sandwiches. She would tell me how unhappy she was at home...not allowed to do this or that, or to go to discos and parties in town or on holiday with her friends... she would cry and nestle into me."

"Go on," encouraged the detective.

"Well, she smelt so good with deodorant or was it perfume and she seemed so distressed, I put my arm around her to comfort her, she raised her head and kissed my cheek. I pulled away; I knew I was getting caught up in her enchanting manoeuvres on me. It seemed that she wasn't the innocent 15 year old girl sat enticing me, but a beautiful woman crying out to be loved! ... Nothing further happened that day."

"When did it happen?" the detective asked.

"I can't remember the date, but I know I was developing real deep feelings for her, she was so beautiful and full of life, I fell in love with her and was easily led on. I know, I know I'm old enough to be her father and should know better, but she made me feel so young again, so alive! I loved her laugh and her antics she would get up to. She was such a joy to be with… then one day we seemed very excited with each other's company. I'd pulled over into a layby for lunch, we got out, but lunch wasn't on her mind! …she grabbed my hand and led me to the side door of the horse trailer and we went inside. I couldn't control the event; I was just swept along on this tide of unrealism. I really needed her comfort and the love she wanted to give, I'd been so lonely and depressed after Letty died. Carla filled the void that was left inside me. She encouraged me to lay down, I was so weak, it was if she had me under her spell, we made love, I was gentle as I could. She told me how much she loved me and wanted to spend the rest of her life with me!"

"What did you say?" asked the detective.

"I was too overwhelmed to say anything! I'd never had anyone express their love for me so expressively and unwavering like that before! Afterwards I felt ashamed, I should have known better but at the time it was exhilarating and truly wonderful, I didn't want it to end."

He placed his large hands around his ruddy cheeks, his eyes stared down at the dark brown carpet on the floor. The detectives allowed him to pause for a while before the next question.

"Did you have sex on other occasions?"

Steve was annoyed. "I wouldn't call it just sex! It was much more than that, it was true love for her, I really loved her! I still love her with all my heart. No, we didn't make love again, we decided we wouldn't do it again until she was 16, it was very hard for both of us. I've written to her but there has been no reply, her parents have probably intercepted my letters. I know she still loves me."

"Why did you run?" asked the lead detective.

Steve continued talking but he spoke more quickly with a nervous tone. "I wasn't running away from Carla! ... She told me she was two months pregnant. Under different circumstances I would have loved a child and especially with Carla... but my world had fallen apart. I knew her parents wouldn't approve or the villagers, I would have taken Carla with me but that would probably have been classed as kidnap, I was scared, very scared... not of being done for under-age sex but terrified of what 'they' would do to me."

"Who are they?" asked the lead detective, puzzled.

"The Black Order," Steve replied, terrified and shaking at the mere mention of their sinister name. "I've said enough, I should never have told you anything, I've been sworn to secrecy, I will be killed for this or worse."

The detectives appeared surprised at Steve's terrified reaction. "We will let you have a break and a drink but you do need to tell us the whole story, we can give you protection where necessary if you are in any danger."

Steve was taken back to the custody cell. He sat down and cried, his delicate emotions were in turmoil, he was so frightened what his future might hold. His hands trembled; he knew he would go to prison for under-age sex, theft of Mrs Redford-Hamilton's property and the disposal of the bodies. It was after he was released that he was most concerned about – would 'they' come looking for him and castrate him or even kill him for his wicked crime? If 'they' found out he had given their names to the police, he would definitely be killed in a torturous way!

The detectives arrived at the incident room to discuss the investigation surrounding Cathy Reed. It had been confirmed that the decomposing body on the embankment with the rucksack was definitely Cathy Reed. Her post-mortem had revealed her hyoid bone was broken – this occurs in about 50% of strangulation and 27% in hangings.

"We know she was dropped off at the church in Deadend village and she was going to the bell tower. The bell rope found in the mud was the same colours as the bell ropes in the bell tower at Deadend village."

"She could have been hanged there," the younger detective suggested.

"Or she came upon a hanging - Mrs Redford-Hamilton perhaps…was Cathy Reed strangled to eliminate her as a witness?"

"What about Christine Holmes? … She must have met Cathy Reed in that small timeframe, in the bell tower."

The lead detective pondered for a moment and replied, "I think we will have another chat with our vicar, see if we can find out a bit more about bell ropes."

The detectives drove up the lonely country road to Deadend village. The buds were beginning to open on the tree branches, spring was finally on its way. They arrived at The New Vicarage, and parked behind the vicar's car on the driveway. The detective knocked loudly on the door. There was no reply so they knocked again. The lead detective was annoyed; he was expecting him to be there. They walked around the house looking through the windows and banging on the back door.

"He's not in – we'll go to the church, he may be there, he can't be very far away, his car's still here."

They opened the main church door with the huge, heavy circular, iron door handle. They heard giggling female voices inside. A group of women were cleaning the church pews; they had spray bottles and dusters in their hands.

"Do you know where we can find the vicar?" the younger detective asked.

"We haven't seen him all day, which is most unusual," one of the women replied.

"Are any of you bell ringers?" asked the lead detective on the off chance he might get some answers.

Mildred spoke up in her usual cheerful voice, "Yes I'm a bell ringer."

"Do you keep spare bell ropes?"

"Yes, we do, just in case we need to replace one," Mildred replied, surprised at the question.

The lead detective continued with the questioning. "Who replaces them?"

"Well, I used to do it but I'm too old now so the vicar usually changes them. If we order a full set and have them all changed at once, someone from town does it."

The lead detective asked, "Did you notice if one of the bell ropes was suddenly replaced last August on 29th, for no apparent reason?"

Mildred thought for a moment. "I think we changed all the bell ropes mid-August last year, so no I wouldn't notice a new one. They were all new."

"Do you know if a spare one is missing?"

"I can have a look; we usually keep them in the storeroom, follow me." Mildred led them through the second door on the right near the vestry. She took a box down from a shelf and opened it. The room was full of boxes and stone statues; in the corner was a tall artificial Christmas tree. There was a large rusty iron clapper laid on the floor – the ball and shaft that swings inside the bell – it looked very heavy.

"Well, I could have sworn there were two spare bell ropes in here but there's only one now!" Mildred exclaimed in surprise.

The detectives thanked her and left, then headed to 1 Fell Houses where the organist Bill Dobson lived. They knew he was the vicar's lover – perhaps he would know where the vicar was.

They rang the doorbell at the front door, but there was no reply. They walked around the house, peering in through the windows; around the back they saw both the vicar and Bill Dobson sat on the settee in a back room, they appeared to be asleep. They banged on the window but there was no movement. Suspicious, they broke in and ran to the motionless pair. The vicar still had his vicar's dog collar on but was dressed casually like his partner. Their faces were pale and lifeless.

The lead detective tried to feel for a pulse on the vicar's neck; the other detective did the same with Bill Dobson. They both looked at each other and shook their heads.

"A suicide pact," the lead detective announced. He was very disappointed but moved – they must have loved each other dearly to go to such extremes. He picked up the empty bottle of tablets sat on the coffee table. There was also an empty bottle of whisky, together with two empty shot glasses. He notified the coroner via his mobile phone.

"I think the vicar had something to hide besides his homosexual relationship with Bill Dobson. It must have been when he heard we had found the body of Cathy Reed. He had something to do with all this business at the bell tower, I know it. I hope Steve Mann is going to 'spill the beans' or we will never know!"

The house soon quickly filled up with people examining and assessing the scene. It was confirmed as a double suicide; there was no evidence to suggest it was a homicide. The two bodies were removed in body bags and were taken to the mortuary for the pathologist to examine.

****

Word quickly spread throughout the village about the cars and commotion at Bill Dobson's house. In the village hall, a group of women were setting up a children's art exhibition ready for the judges, to award prizes that evening. There was going to be a presentation of silver cups to the winners of each age group.

"They've committed suicide!" cried Milly when she heard the depressing news; she burst into tears. "The vicar was a lovely man, why would he do such a thing!"

Mrs Ackroyd had no feelings at all. "I tried to tell you they were gay but no one would believe me, so now you know!" She stormed off in her usual huff.

"I don't care if they were gay, they didn't need to do this, they were both well liked, it didn't matter if they were having a homosexual relationship, they were discreet about it," Jenny cried out, tears running down her cheeks. She would miss the vicar at bell ringing practice and his enjoyable and sometimes humorous church services. He even used to take part in the church plays, usually as the character of a bumbling vicar!

****

Steve Mann was brought in to the interview room for further questioning. He looked around the small quiet room and sat in a chair at the table. He had decided he didn't want a solicitor, the fewer people that know about the tales of Deadend village the better.

"I'm sorry to inform you, the vicar and Bill Dobson, the organist, have committed suicide this morning at Bill's house."

Steve was totally stunned; they were his friends and his only allies in this mess. He tried to compose himself, the best he could.

"Why do you think they committed suicide? Did they have anything to do with The Black Order, or the three women disappearing on 29th August 2018?" the lead detective asked. He was scrutinizing his face for any signs of lying.

"My life is in real danger if I mention anything, I've already said too much. If I tell you all I know, will you drop all charges to the under-age sex case?" Steve pleaded.

"We don't have the authority to drop your case, only a judge can do that. We will of course inform the judge of your full cooperation on the case of the three women and it will then be his decision."

"OK, I'll tell you what I know but I want full police protection." Steve was terrified at what could happen to him.

"We can grant you protection if your life is in danger," the lead detective promised, eager to sew up this case once and for all.

Steve began to talk in a shaky voice. "The Black Order was formed in 1635 long before police were around. It was founded because a villager had gone berserk, rampaging through the village murdering men, women, children and babies with a bill hook knife, one of the tools of his trade, he was the local woodsman. It was called 'the massacre of 1635'. The guilty man was strapped to an iron gate and laid horizontally over posts' supports. Each villager eagerly packed bundles of wood underneath. The wood was lit and they burnt him alive, his blood-curdling screams were heard for miles, they said." Steve shuffled uncomfortably in his chair and continued in a low voice.

"The elders of the village were sworn in as members of The Black Order; it was kept a secret from the rest of the villagers. Each member passed on their role to their son or sons, nothing was written down, knowledge was verbally passed on, that was the rule, everything was a secret even from their wives. If anyone stepped out of line on this, it was a swift death and a cover up. Villagers were presented at the secret Black Order's Court, if they had committed very serious offences, that's why the members wore the black cloaks and masks to hide their identity – it always meant death to the accused as no one was allowed to go free after meeting The Black Order."

"You must be a member, then, to know all this?" asked the younger detective intrigued at this secret society and the grizzly history of the village.

"Yes, my father and grandfather prepared me for the role as did their fathers and grandfathers before them."

The lead detective asked, "What was your purpose?"

Steve replied, "To protect the village and keep it thriving."

"How often do you meet and where?"

"We only meet once a year now, on the 1st August, in the vicar's attic, we wear black cloaks and masks only for its tradition for the occasion. We generally discuss the behaviour of any villager who we think are heading into a life of crime and try and alter their ways to prevent another massacre; it's mainly just tradition now. The villagers are mostly law abiding and many still go to church."

That explains the black cloaks and full faced black leather masks that they had found during the search at The New Vicarage, thought the lead detective.

"Who else is a member of The Black Order?" Steve was asked.

Steve hesitated for a while; he knew he was breaking all the rules if he breathed a word of this. He desperately hoped the police would keep their promise of police protection.

"The vicar or his real name is Daniel Cramner. The organist as you know is Bill Dobson. Craig Ruddy, John Milton, John Kiln and Ken Robinson."

"Craig Ruddy is the artist, isn't he?" asked the young detective sounding very surprised.

"Yes, John Milton is the solicitor, John Kiln is married to Jenny Kiln and Ken Robinson is Carla Robinson's father."

"I see now why you are so frightened; Ken Robinson is furious with you for your part in his young daughter's pregnancy, he'll know it's a criminal offence to perform under-age sex. What punishment would The Black Order carry out on you?"

"I would probably be castrated or worse and may even be slowly tortured to death." Steve leaned over and cupped his large hands around his fearful face and murmured, "My grandfather told me of an older man who was the sworn enemy of one of the members of The Black Order; he got his young daughter pregnant on purpose to anger him; little did he know the father was a member of the secret Black Order this was in the 1700s. Out of revenge, The Black Order stripped and gagged him; his hands were bound behind his back. He was hung naked upside down from a beam and his private parts were hacked off! He suffered 100 slash wounds all over his body, from the knives each member used. They all counted each inflicted wound one by one… He slowly and agonizingly bled to death!" Steve's colour drained from his face and he began to shake uncontrollably.

"Surely they wouldn't do anything like that in this day and age! That's barbaric!" the young detective exclaimed in a sudden unexpected outburst.

"That solicitor and his cronies, John Kiln, Ken Robinson and Craig Ruddy, are quite capable of anything! Me, Bill Dobson and the vicar are the good guys."

"Who's in charge of this organization?"

"No one, we work as a team, all decisions are democratically voted for. The problem is me, Bill and the vicar are outvoted every time by that solicitor and his three cronies."

They were suddenly interrupted by a knock at the door. A police officer hurried in with a note in his hand. The lead detective read the note and left urgently. The other detective closed down the interview. Steve was relieved when he was taken back to his custody cell. He wondered how all this mess was going to end and if he still had a future. He thought about his love for Carla and their unborn child, he knew he had left her in the lurch but under the circumstances, he hadn't any other choice – he had to run for his life!

The following morning, Steve Mann dressed as smartly as he could. He was taken to court to appear before the judge for his crime of under-age sex. It was a modern courthouse with a large airy courtroom. He confirmed his details to the judge and also pleaded guilty. He was taken away after his 10-minute appearance. The police drove him back to the police headquarters.

THE GRUESOME FIND

The lead detective had rushed to the local hospital – the note had informed him that his wife was unconscious after a road accident in her car. He was extremely relieved when he was told that she was now fully conscious and had only minor injuries. She would be staying in the hospital overnight for observations.

Steve Mann was taken to the interview room, when the lead detective arrived back the following day to the police headquarters. Steve was unaware of the trauma the detective had experienced. After the introductions for the recording, the lead detective continued: "We will begin with your account of The Black Order's meeting on the 1st August 2018. Which members attended and what was discussed at that meeting?"

Steve thought for a while and told him, "There was myself, the vicar, Bill Dobson, Craig Ruddy, John Milton, John Kiln and Ken Robinson present at that meeting. The vicar had informed the group, he was concerned about the complaints about Mrs Redford-Hamilton, villagers were outraged at the way she treated them and how she was taking over clubs. A few other members there, joined in and said the same."

"Was there anything else that was mentioned?" the younger detective asked.

"Yes, come to think of it, at that particular meeting Craig Ruddy confessed he was having an affair with Wendy Stubbs! We were all a bit flabbergasted; it wasn't an offence of course. He would have been severely punished if it was. Craig had brought the blackmail letter as proof, he wanted it kept a secret within the group. We all read the typed letter and asked if he had paid the money; he told us he had. We all thought it could only be Mrs Redford-Hamilton but we hadn't any proof. We were not sure how to handle this arrogant, domineering woman, but the vicar volunteered to have a quiet word with her. He said, he would tell her she was upsetting the villagers by taking away their roles in the clubs and that she should work more as a team."

The lead detective asked Steve if they had had another meeting before 29th August 2018.

"Yes! We did call an urgent meeting, on the evening of the 28th. Things were getting out of hand. We heard Mrs Redford-Hamilton had been accused of shooting Jack and Susy's dog and had poisoned Gail's cat! We also heard from John Milton, the solicitor, confessing to having an affair with Kate Brown, his secretary – they'd both been separately blackmailed with demands for money. We were shocked, we all thought he wasn't the type to have an affair! He told us, he and Kate had also paid £1000 each."

"Were there anymore confessions?" asked the young detective.

Steve Mann continued, "It didn't really come as a shock when the vicar also confessed. We all sort of knew he was having a homosexual relationship with Bill Dobson. He told us he had been blackmailed as well. He was clever though, he had hidden and watched from the bell ringer's room. He had waited for the blackmailer to pick up the £1000 in the plastic bag which he'd placed behind the old gravestone at the back of the graveyard. He saw through the window; it was Mrs Redford-Hamilton. We decided she had gone too far this time; we would arrange a meeting with her and have it out with her."

"Where did this meeting take place?" asked the lead detective, captivated in what he was hearing; he was excited that the case would soon be wrapped up.

"The vicar made the excuse to her that a few people were having a meeting in the bell tower, to discuss what to do about the jackdaws pushing sticks through the slats in the window. Something she had complained about on many occasions, so he knew she would come to take over the meeting."

"When did this meeting take place?" he was asked.

"On the 29th August 2018 at 1.15 pm."

"Go on, tell us what happened."

"We decided not to wear our cloaks and masks, I was to lock the church door when she was in the bell ringing room, to stop anyone coming in and interrupting our meeting. It was a Wednesday so villagers would be busy in the village hall all day, so we were hoping no one would bang on the door wanting to be let in!" Steve paused to get his breath. "There was the vicar, John Milton and Craig Ruddy waiting for her up the steps, I joined them later."

166

"What did she say when she saw all you lot there?" asked the young detective.

"She said, 'it doesn't take this many to decide what to do, it was just a question of who was going to put up the mesh required to stop the sticks being pushed through the slats'. John Milton revealed to her, she had been asked to come here to discuss her conduct towards the villagers and about the blackmailing."

"What did she say?" asked the lead detective. He was becoming more and more absorbed in this interview.

"She screamed out, 'How dare you ask me to come here under false pretences and don't talk to me in that tone of voice! I've done nothing wrong.' The list of things she had done were reeled off to her, she was told the vicar had witnessed her collecting his money behind the gravestone. She looked very angry, like a cornered rat and astounded at being exposed for what she was!"

"Then what happened?"

"We argued with her, we could see her becoming more and more enraged, her eyes were flashing fury at us! Suddenly, she pulled out her metal hair comb from her hair and lunged at John Milton with it, aiming at his jugular in his neck! She hated the solicitor because he always stood up to her, she'd certainly met her match with him." Steve gave a little laugh. "We all rushed towards her but the solicitor pushed her violently backwards with such force, she lost her balance, staggered backwards and fell down the wooden stairs! It all happened so quick!" Steve nervously bit the corner of his first fingernail.

"Was she dead?" he was asked.

"We ran down the steps horrified, the solicitor took her pulse, there was nothing! We thought she must have broken her neck in the fall, there was no blood!"

"What did you do with her body?"

"The vicar thought we should ring the police and say we just found her lying there, it would appear to be an accident, she had just lost her footing and fell to her death. We voted on it as John Milton wanted to dispose of the body. He said, 'if the police come they will be in her house and find evidence of her blackmailing us, we would still be accused of murder, my life in the village would be finished and probably my career!' He was furious with her."

"How did everyone vote?"

"The vicar and I voted to ring the police, John Milton and Craig Ruddy voted to dispose of the body, it was a 50/50 split. John Milton told us that we had no choice and demanded we did what he wanted. John and Craig immediately lifted the body up and walked towards the vestry. The vicar and I were disgusted and outraged, the vicar said he would go and get a torch and get a cloak and mask as well. I think he wanted to bury her in some kind of shroud and give her some dignity. I picked up the metal hair comb and followed the others."

Steve Mann wiped his forehead with the back of his hand; he was sweating profusely. The memories of the anxiety and guilt were tearing him apart. "Her mobile phone and house keys were removed from her pocket in her cardigan, I tucked the hair comb back into her hair. Her body was wrapped in the black cloak. The secret door in the vestry was opened, John and Craig carried her in. I shone the torch to light the way, as it was pitch black in there and very cold. The second heavy door was opened with a key the vicar had."

"We will have to obtain that key," the young detective remarked. "Continue," he urged.

"There were stones steps to negotiate with the body. They laid her on a stone shelf, it's in a kind of alcove. The vicar stood beside her and said a prayer and laid the black mask over her face. We shut the doors and had a meeting in the vestry. We decided to remove all evidence of the blackmailing from her house that night."

"Tell me more about this secret room," the lead detective asked.

"It's not a room, it's a tunnel, it connects The Old Vicarage to the church, it's about 200 feet in length, it used to come out in the secret room, I think it's a broom cupboard now. The tunnel was bricked up and boarded in the broom cupboard when The Old Vicarage went up for sale. Only The Black Order know about the tunnel."

"So, you left the body in the tunnel and had a meeting in the vestry – then what happened?"

"We heard screams from the church, the vicar told us he had forgotten to lock the church door when he returned with the cloak, mask and torch. We all went into the church. A middle-aged woman was running towards us shouting there's a body hanging from a bell rope! We were all totally stunned! We couldn't believe our ears! Two dead bodies in one day! Unbelievable! The woman was screaming at us to ring the police, we were paralysed with fear for a moment. We couldn't call the police; we didn't want cops crawling all over the place. The vicar decided to take the middle-aged woman out of the church; he was probably thinking that John Milton would kill her too, to shut her up!"

Steve took a sip of water from his glass while the detectives watched trying to work out if this was all correct with the timeline they knew about. They had estimated that Cathy Reed – on the end of the rope – arrived at about 2 pm, Christine Holmes at about 2.30 pm, which would fit in with his explanation.

Steve continued, "I ran up the bell tower steps with the others, there before us was a woman, perhaps in her 30s hanging limp from a makeshift noose around her neck she'd made using the bell rope. We ran over, but she was dead as a doornail. She had used one of the chairs, she'd placed it on a wooden box. She had obviously climbed onto the chair, made the slip knot and slipped the noose around her neck and kicked the chair over. Poor soul she was desperate to part from this world for some reason… The bell rope was solid, you know – not going up and down as normal. We suspected she knew about bell ropes and had fixed the bell in the belfry in order to hang herself and also not to ring the bell to alert anyone. I went up into the belfry to see, I released the rope after the others had removed the body from the noose so as not to ring the bell. We decided to take her body to the vestry and wrap her and her rucksack up in some black plastic sheeting there. There was no more room in the tunnel, it was a very narrow tunnel with only the one shelf, so we thought we would dispose of her that night. John Milton said we should change the bell rope in case there was any of her DNA left on it."

"So, who changed the bell rope?" asked the lead detective.

"It was arranged the vicar would change the bell rope, he was the only one of us who knew how, he was also to dispose of it. John Milton had an important meeting that evening so it was up to me and Craig Ruddy to dispose of the body."

"We have found the body and the bell rope," the young detective informed him.

"I thought you must have," Steve answered nervously.

"What did you do with the black plastic sheeting around the body?" asked the lead detective.

"It was thrown away in the recycling bin in the town as it had our fingerprints on it."

"What was your intention regarding a punishment for Mrs Redford-Hamilton's conduct?"

"We were going to threaten her with going to the police, proving she was a blackmailer. We had told her the vicar had witnessed her picking up the money. John Milton said, 'if you don't agree to move out of the village, then we will inform the police about the blackmailing.' He was very threatening with her," Steve answered looking nervously at the detective.

"What did she say to that?"

"She wasn't in the least bit scared, she said in her haughty, arrogant voice – 'You wouldn't dare put your reputations at risk, it would all come out in the newspapers and on the television, you would all be totally exposed of your shameful sordid affairs, you disgusting people! You are all buffoons!'… She knew how to handle us!"

"So, what did you do then?" asked the young detective.

"John Milton said, in his loud threatening, solicitor's voice, 'if you don't move out of the village willingly, we have ways to remove you permanently!' Mrs Redford-Hamilton gasped; she knew she would be murdered if she didn't go. It was then she lunged at him with her metal hair comb!"

"When were the items taken from The Old Vicarage, now that your evening was full with disposing of the body and bell rope?"

"We all met up at midnight, the four of us, we went around the back through the boot room, we had her keys from her pocket to get in. We all wore gloves so as not to leave any fingerprints. We found her camera and tape recorder in her desk drawer which was locked. Craig Ruddy used his penknife to release the lock. We took her computer as her blackmailing letters would have been typed on it and would be still in the computer's memory somewhere. John Milton found all the copies she had kept of the blackmailing letters and copies of the explicit photos in a box file on the shelf."

"What about the spade with her initials engraved on the wooden shaft – who took that and where is it now?"

"I took that from the shed, I threw it into undergrowth on the way back from disposing of the body."

"Where did you dump the mobile phone and her house keys?"

"Craig threw them in the lake," answered Steve as he fumbled in his pocket for a handkerchief.

"Why didn't you bury the body at the site where the bell rope was buried?"

Steve glanced up and replied, "The vicar disposed of the bell rope after he replaced it with a new one, that's what we'd agreed on. Craig and I tried to dispose of the body somewhere else but it was really hard digging, the mud was very heavy and sticky after the rain. We dug so far down then decided to take the body elsewhere. We couldn't find anywhere suitable to dig another grave, so we rolled her into the undergrowth down the embankment out of sight. We had to get back by midnight."

"What did you do with the items from the house?"

"We stored them in one of the storerooms at the church, the vicar took the box file and burnt all the papers and photos on his open fire; he must have done the same with the box file. The hard drive on the computer was removed and hammered into pieces. The memory card from the camera was also destroyed that night. After damaging the other items, they were all taken to the dump in the town as damaged goods. We used different days by different people so as not to cause suspicion."

"So, you thought you had done the perfect crime!" the lead detective exclaimed, smiling. He knew that without Steve Mann's help the case would never have been solved.

"Yes, we thought we had covered our tracks well," Steve replied.

"Tell us about the middle-aged woman that the vicar took out of the church."

"He told us later he had taken her into the meeting room at The New Vicarage. He had given her some sugary tea and covered her biscuit with LSD powder – he knew if he didn't get her out of the village, madman John Milton would murder her. The vicar was desperate to keep her alive, she was just in the wrong place at the wrong time but knew too much. The vicar thought she would just have a pleasant LSD trip which would cloud her memory and give the whole event she'd witnessed an unreal feeling, so she wouldn't be a credible witness. He hadn't realized that because she was in a heightened state of stress, the LSD would give her a bad trip. He was mortified when he found out she had careered off the road and drowned in the lake. No one will know what horrors her drugged up mind must have conjured up for her. The vicar was distraught about it all, he felt so devastated with guilt, we knew he was thinking about committing suicide. Bill Dobson and I helped him out of his depression."

"Give us a timeline after the bodies were disposed of, when did you find out from Carla Robinson she's pregnant?" asked the lead detective.

Steve pondered for a few seconds. "It was roughly two months later, at the end of October when I found out from Carla about her pregnancy, I was the first she had told. It was that night I packed up and left the village, I was terrified for my life. The Black Order only punished you if you've broken the law, which I had. I've had nightmares since about if they found me and what they would do to me, especially that madman John Milton!"

"It's very late, we will finish the interview and take you to the church tomorrow. You can show us how to open the secret door into the tunnel and show us where Mrs Redford-Hamilton's body was laid to rest."

Warrants had been applied for, to arrest the other men involved – John Milton, the solicitor and Craig Ruddy the artist for their part in disposing of the bodies, of Cathy

Reed hanging in the bell ringer's room and Mrs Redford-Hamilton.

****

In the village hall that night, a group of people were clearing up.

"Someone saw Steve Mann in a police car in town heading towards the police station!" Rachel had announced. She was a member of the historical society club. Rachel and the others were stacking the chairs away, after the evening talk about 'The history of the great plague of 1665 in the area'.

"They've got Steve Mann then? They'll have arrested him on charges of under-age sex, the perverted man. It must have been him that got Carla Robinson pregnant – they were always together at weekends," came the reply.

Rachel continued, "He'll be out in a couple of years, Carla will have come to her senses by then and found a lad more suitable for her age, to marry."

"Carla's parents would never allow her to marry Steve, he's too old!" exclaimed another. The chairs scraped loudly on the wooden floor as they were pushed to the sides of the hall.

Sam pondered out loud – "I wonder when they will find Mrs Redford-Hamilton, she must be dead somewhere."

The others laughed. "We hope she's dead, we don't want her coming back here and upsetting our way of life anymore!" one of them blurted out.

****

There was an early morning raid on the homes of the men involved in the disposing of the two bodies. John Milton was arrested before he went to work at his solicitor's office in the town, Craig Ruddy was also arrested at his cottage. They were taken in separate police cars to the police headquarters and questioned in separate interview rooms.

Both claimed they knew absolutely nothing about 'The Black Order' or about any bodies. They both said that Steve Mann had made the whole thing up to cover up his own involvement in the crimes; they blamed him for the three women disappearing.

The detectives escorted Steve Mann to the old church in Deadend village. Steve was pleased he was out of his cell and in the fresh air, he was glad to see the old village again. He wondered how Carla was coping – if only she knew he was only about a mile away from her at the church. He knew it would never be safe to see her again.

He showed the detectives how to open the secret door in the vestry using a lever hidden under a ledge. They all walked into a small area with their torches switched on. The tiny room was built with stone with a vaulted stone ceiling.

They saw a heavy wooden inner door before them. The large ring handle was turned with a handkerchief but the door was locked. The lead detective produced a large key from his jacket pocket – the key had been found in the vicar's trouser pocket. The stale air wafted in their faces as the heavy door was swung open; there was a faint smell of rotting flesh, the odour of death!

"Now mind yourselves, there's 12 stone steps down into the tunnel, I'll go first as I can show you where she is," Steve told them, shining his torch on the dusty steps.

They walked in single file through the low, narrow tunnel, their torch lights showing them the way, deeper into the tunnel.

"How much further is it?" asked the young detective. He felt uneasy and surprised at how long the tunnel was.

"We are nearly there… oh my gosh!" cried Steve Mann who was leading them.

"What is it?" cried the young detective at the back.

"She's gone!" screamed Steve, the hair on the back of his neck stood up! The torch light lit the empty stone shelf in the alcove.

They all stared at the empty space trying to comprehend why the body of Mrs Redford-Hamilton had been moved.

"Did the others move her out of here?" asked the disappointed lead detective. He was hoping there would be DNA present from John Milton and Craig Ruddy on her clothing proving they had been involved.

"No, no one has moved her, not that I know of, there was nowhere else to put her!" Steve cried, knowing full well they were not believing a word he was saying now.

The torch light shone on the black leather mask lying on the stone flagged floor below the alcove. The lead detective picked it up.

"Well, it looks like you were telling the truth, the body has been here, I think, but the others must have moved her when you'd left the village." The detectives knew they were back to square one – without a body and confessions from John Milton and Craig Ruddy they couldn't charge them.

Steve Mann was returned to his custody cell. As they drove down the road from the church, he could see the fields were greening up with spring grass. They pulled into a layby to let Milly pass by in her car. He looked away – he felt ashamed sitting in a police car. He wondered what the villagers were saying about him, had they labelled him a paedophile? He knew he could never live in Deadend village ever again.

The detectives had been waiting for the results of the forensic analysis to be completed on Cathy Reed's clothes and rucksack, and the results had finally arrived. The detectives were eager to see the results – hair had been found on Cathy's jeans and unknown DNA was present, it hadn't matched any DNA on the database.

Unknown fingerprints had also been found on the inside of her plastic belt that was holding up her jeans. They had assumed these had been left, when the men lifted Cathy's body up by her legs to release the noose around her neck, then lain her down on the floor.

John Milton and Craig Ruddy had willingly had their cheeks swabbed for DNA and their fingerprints were taken, not realizing they had left crucial evidence at the scene.

It was found the hair belonged to John Milton and the fingerprints belonged to Craig Ruddy. When the two men were confronted with the evidence, they eventually confessed to everything.

They knew they would go to prison for their involvement, but by confessing to theft and disposing of the bodies, they hoped to gain a shorter sentence.

They were both relieved that Carla's father, Ken Robinson, and John Kiln would carry on with their duties for The Black Order. Steve Mann would never be safe especially if he wanted to marry and live with Carla and their baby after his prison term.

"Where did you take Mrs Redford-Hamilton's body after it was laid on the stone shelf in the secret tunnel?" demanded the lead detective to John Milton and Craig Ruddy, in their separate interviews.

Each of the men looked puzzled. Both of them told the detectives that the body was never moved again, unless the vicar and his partner Bill Dobson had moved it at a later date.

The detectives decided to take Steve Mann back into the tunnel. They walked through the tunnel by the light from their torches, the sickening smell of death was everywhere. Their torch light lit the empty shelf as they passed by.

"How much further to the end of the tunnel?" asked the young detective. He hated small dark spaces, he felt queasy, claustrophobic and very scared.

"About another 100 feet," replied Steve.

They had covered their nostrils with handkerchiefs, the smell was unbearable. At the end of the tunnel at The Old Vicarage, the stench was even stronger. The light from Steve's torch lit up a black mass on the stone flagged floor by another heavy inner wooden door.

"That's her in the black cloak!" cried Steve, his eyes bulging with shock and fear. They all thought the vicar must have moved her there for some reason.

The lead detective bent down and lifted the black cloak; the body was in an awful state of decomposition. With his handkerchief tightly around his nose he lifted up her blackened, partially mummified hands, one at a time. The torch light revealed her broken nails and cut finger; her knuckles showed massive abrasions. The inside of her hands were also cut. There were tiny splinters of wood in her fingertips and on the outer rim of her palms of her hands.

"She was a live!" gasped the lead detective getting up quickly, alarmed and stepping back into the other detective. "She must have regained consciousness and flung the mask off her face. In the pitch black she must have got off the stone shelf and fumbled her way up to this end of the tunnel and found this heavy door!" exclaimed the shocked detective. He had never experienced anything like this in his long career.

The young detective was shocked and felt sick to the stomach. "I wonder if she thought she was in some kind of catacombs with dead bodies laid on similar shelves, it must have been absolutely terrifying to wake up in here in total darkness! She must have been frantically banging and scratching at the door to get those wounds on her hands, I imagine she'd be screaming for hours at the top of her voice for help. She would have felt utterly distraught and a sense of hopelessness and in total despair, I know I would have!"

The torch was shone at the heavy door for conformation of the scratch marks – there were 100s of desperate scratches and traces of her dried blood.

"No one would have heard her as her house was empty at the time; her relatives didn't arrive until six months later. It's too far away for her screams to have been heard in the church, especially with the other two doors sealed shut at the other end! She probably didn't realize there were two exits to this tunnel. It's such a shame she was probably only a couple of feet from her own broom cupboard!"

Steve asked, "How long would it have taken for her to die?"

The lead detective answered in a solemn voice, "Without food and water, probably about a week at the very most but in these conditions, lack of fresh air, the cold, the extreme stress and anguish and the pitch black it could have been a lot shorter. The pathologist will be able to tell us more details."

The lead detective thought she had probably got her just deserts. He pondered about her crimes, the list of cruelty to animals, the possibility of as many as three people murdered and the attempted murder of Kitty, the forged will and all the blackmailing and bullying.

Steve was troubled, she was a wicked woman but did she really deserve such a horrific, slow, agonizing death in this lonely miserable place in total blackness? He didn't know the full extent of her crimes. He wondered if she had repented of her sins, she must have thought she had arrived in some sort of hell. A deep shudder went all the way down his spine – he knew she would never rest in peace.

Only two mourners, dressed in black, attended Mrs Redford-Hamilton's funeral in the town. Lotty, her daughter, and Ann, her cousin – her only living relatives left who had actually known her.

***

Printed in Great Britain
by Amazon